ANASTASIA

A. MARIE

LIMITLESS PUBLISHING

Anastasia

First Print Edition: December 2018

Limitless Publishing, LLC

Kailua, HI 96734

www.limitlesspublishing.com

Formatting: Limitless Publishing

ISBN-13: 978-1-954194-19-9

❀ Created with Vellum

Dedication: To all of my readers who have supported me and encouraged me to follow my every dream.

ACKNOWLEDGMENTS

Thank you, Daniela and Athena, for helping me with all that you do. I don't think any of my dreams with publishing and getting my name out there would ever come true without the two of you. You both continue to believe in me and inspire me in so many ways. You both are truly my family, and I don't know what I would do without you.

Thank you to all of my friends. Also, a huge thank you to all of my beta readers, my Street Team, my ARC, who volunteer their time in order to help me. I will never forget every single person who goes out of their way to better me.

As for my readers who support my every work, I love you so much. The messages I receive from you and the amount of love I get melts my heart every day. It is so great knowing that all I have to do is open my emails on a bad day, and you all will make it better again. Thank you most, truly.

PROLOGUE

VALENTINO

*A*s I held my weeping baby brother in my arms, I could only stare out at the mess. The blood and dead bodies were littered in front of me, breaking my heart. The faces of my pregnant mother and my stepfather would be burned into my memory forever. I was going to have a sister—our family was going to be complete. Then, in just a blink of an eye, they were gone, leaving me with my younger half-brother, Vincenzo.

I could still remember sitting there at the kitchen table eating my favorite soup. My mother had the most beautiful smile on her face as she talked about the weather outside. She loved the rain, she loved everything it represented. As she went on and on about the old times when she would go outside and play in the rain all on her own, I rolled my eyes. Her words were strange, but I wished I could take it all back now. I wished I would have paid more attention and asked more questions to keep that smile on my mother's face, but I didn't. I ignored her.

Everything happened way too fast. My mother let out this loud piercing scream as the doors slammed open. Men charged in with guns and Mama ran over to me, trying to do everything in her power to protect me. Roberto always told me that women come first. We were to always protect the women in our family, but I didn't protect the woman who meant the most to me. I didn't protect her as they shot her right between the eyes as she raced over to me. I didn't protect her as they fired bullets into her pregnant belly. I didn't protect her.

Vincenzo finally cried himself to sleep, the stress on his three-year-old mind finally getting to him. I had to hold him tightly as I walked up the stairs and laid him down in our mother's bed. There was a splatter of blood kissing his cheek. It pained me that the blood on my brother's cheek was probably from the gunshot that killed his father as he tried to rush Vincenzo to safety.

I would never forget the look on Roberto's face when he saw my dying mother sprawled upon the ground. His heartbreak and defeat were obvious on every feature.

I wanted to shout and find some way to help my family make it out alive, but I couldn't move. Everything played out from afar as I remained sealed in a box, screaming for some way out.

I could only watch in defeat as the men fired their weapons into my stepfather, who shielded Vincenzo from it all. Even as his last breath was taken, he protected my brother just like I should have done for Mama.

Mama saw the world as beautiful. Even the most depressing things like rain found a way to melt her heart. She died only a few feet in front of me. I could have helped her, but I didn't. I was a punk of a man and Roberto would agree.

Heading into the bathroom, I wet a small towel. When I looked at myself in the mirror, I noticed pieces of my mother all over me. She was the only person I truly loved.

I couldn't even look at myself in the mirror any longer as I walked back into the bedroom to my sleeping baby brother. Pressing the towel against his face, I wiped away every trace of blood. He looked so much like my mother as he slept that it pained me. I was the cause for the loss of the most amazing woman in the world. There would be no other soul as pure as hers, and for that, I deserve to never love again because that is the consequence of being a coward.

"I'm sorry, Enzo, but I promise...I promise I will get him back for everything he took from us, even if it is the last thing I do," I cooed as I ran my hand through his hair.

It was a promise that I meant. I craved to reach into that man's chest and squeeze his heart. Just like me, I wanted his pain to reach a level so high, he would wish I had simply taken his life.

Dmitri Ivanov messed with the *wrong* family.

ANASTASIA

I was prepared to become a woman when I was just a little girl. Childhood vanished before my eyes. That's what happens when you rid someone of love. You open the doors to darkness without letting them realize there could ever be color. I want to say that I blamed my mother, but the only way I could do that was to also blame her mother, and then the mother of her mother.

The heat that escalated through my body only seemed to grow as I tried to ignore it. The longer I tossed and turned, the more the temperature pricked my skin. A sigh escaped my lips as I just laid there in a pit of my sweat, hoping it wasn't affecting my sister as much as it was affecting me.

"Nana," Alex called out from the other side of the room. "Mum didn't pay the electricity bill again, did she?"

"Stay here, I'll figure it out," I whispered before getting up from the mattress.

We weren't fortunate enough to own anything to lift our bed off the ground. We were lucky enough to simply have a mattress.

I walked out of my room and straight to my mother's.

Softly knocking on the door, I waited for a response. It seemed as if long moments passed before the door finally opened to reveal some half naked stranger. He had a small towel to cover up his *area*, but other than that, he was naked. The stench in the room assaulted my nostrils. It didn't help that there was no electricity to help ventilate the area.

"Uh, your Ma's pretty occupied, sweetie," the man said, with a hint of a New York accent. His cornrow braids went down the back of his head, and the cigarette that sat perched at the corner of his mouth added to his whole appeal. What irritated me most was the fact that he talked to me as if I were twelve.

I narrowed my eyes at him before propping my hand on my hip. "I need to speak to my mum."

He let out a groan of annoyance right before closing the door. Seconds later, my mum appeared in all her glory. She was wearing a scowl on her face as she looked at me.

My mum began tying the strings of her robe as she narrowed her eyes at me.

"What the hell do you want, Nana?" she asked, closing the door behind her. Based on the slur of her words, I knew she was high. It was almost as if she couldn't survive a day without a high pushing her to live. I just couldn't identify *what* she could've gotten high from this time. *Was it meth, crack, weed?*

"It's hot. Did you forget to pay the electricity again?" I asked.

"What do you think I'm doing right now? I didn't have the money, okay? He's going to pay me for a good time. That way, I can feed you and your sister. Then, I will get our electricity back on once I have the money," she said, her words coming off almost unrecognizable.

Shaking my head, I grabbed her hand. "You didn't have the money? I made sure I gave you my whole check. Don't tell me you spent it all just to get high!" I seethed. "You are a grown woman; you need to get your priorities straight!"

She narrowed her eyes into slits. I could almost smell how angry she had become in just those few seconds. "You're twenty years old. If you don't like the way we live, then *leave!*"

"You know I have to take care of you and Alex. I can't just leave my little sister. I don't trust the way you are when you have drugs in your system. She's only seventeen, and knowing you, you'd sell her just to get high. You used to be a great mother. Now, you deserve to go to hell," I told her, on the brink of tears.

I knew it was coming as soon as her hand cocked back. My instincts couldn't help but take over as I shut my eyes to prepare for the collision. Pain quickly danced around my skin from the impact of her swing. My head almost knocked off to the side as I held my hand against my cheek. When I looked back at her, grasping my cheek, my jaw seemed to fall as my vision blurred from needy tears.

"Mum!" Alex shrieked. "Why would you hit her?"

At that moment, my mother's bedroom door opened. The previously naked man was now completely dressed. He looked at us before beginning to walk toward our front door. I watched as he shook his head in disapproval.

"Dante, where are you going?" my mother called out before walking toward him.

"I came for a quick fuck. I didn't come to listen to you deal with your crazy family," he said.

My mother grabbed a hold of his wrist, tears falling from her eyes. "Baby, I'm sorry. They'll leave us alone. Please, just don't go. You know how good I made you feel, I could do that again, and whatever else that you want."

He looked at her, rolling his eyes in complete disgust.

"Get off me," he demanded, pushing her as hard as he

could. My sister and I watched as she fell to the floor with a loud thud. My mother quickly got up and attempted to chase after him, but she was too late. The door had already slammed shut.

"Look at what y'all did! I needed the money. I needed it. Goddammit!" she yelled out.

I looked over at Alex to see that her nose was bleeding. The longer I watched her, the quicker I realized that her eyes were shutting as she stared at Mum. I couldn't help but also notice how unevenly her body seemed to sway.

"Alex, are you okay?"

I hurriedly walked over to the restroom, grabbing as much toilet paper as I could. Promptly, I held it up to her nose as my heartbeat seemed to race. My brows were furrowed as hope began banging on the door to my heart that Alex would be okay.

"Nana, I don't feel too good," she whispered. It wasn't the first time she had her nose bleeds. She had been having them for the past few weeks. However, I had never seen her so drained before.

I walked her to the bed, and I helped her lay down. My eyes scanned her body and saw many bruises and red spots. She looked terrible, and with my constant working, it made it challenging to notice any of this.

"We need to take her to a hospital, now!" I exclaimed.

"For a nosebleed? Really, Anastasia? It's probably just the heat," my mum responded, still leaning against the door.

Shaking my head, I walked back over to my sister, placing my hand on her head. She was burning up with a fever.

"I don't think so. I remember her telling me that she has been getting infections like crazy. She hasn't been eating, and look at her arm," I said before grabbing a hold of it to show her all the bruises were appearing on her skin. "Something is wrong with Alex!"

I watched my mother as she walked over to my sister. She did the same thing I did—checked her temperature by raising her hand to her forehead. "I'll get dressed, then I'll start the car, and you have to get her in there. I have things I have to do later, so you're going to have to take care of her. I'll figure out how to pay the electricity bill so it can be on by the time you get back."

Her words were no longer slurred, but I still didn't know if I could trust her to drive.

"I'm not high, I swear. I was just a little tipsy," she told me. It wasn't like I had much of a choice, so I just turned away from her and focused on Alex. Her eyes were closed as she laid on the bed. The warmth wasn't helping her at all, it only supported the drained look she had.

"Alex, do you think you're okay to stand up?" I asked her, biting down on my lip. She nodded her head before moving to get back on her two feet. I helped her off the mattress before grabbing her socks and shoes. Placing them on her feet, I let her lean against me as we walked out of our small apartment and down the stairs.

There were a few times when she came close to missing a step, but I was there to make sure she didn't fall. When we finally made it to the bottom, my mother was in the car, but she seemed distracted, talking on the phone. I didn't pay her any attention as I opened the back door and carefully laid Alexandria down on it.

My mum abruptly let herself out of the car, slamming the door behind her. There was an apologetic look marring her features.

"Dante is coming back, so I can't drop you guys off. I'm sorry, baby girl, but I need the money. When you guys come back and Alex is all well, the electricity will be back on. I love you guys, okay? I really do," she rushed, before throwing the keys toward me and walking back upstairs.

I stared at her disappearing figure with disappointment filling me like it had done so many times before. When it came to my mother, disappointment was her best friend. They walked, ran, and got high together. Disappointment loomed in my soul every time I thought for a second that my mother loved us as much as she said she does. That was what my mother was to me…nothing but a disappointment.

It wasn't her fault, though, that she chose money over her daughter. I blamed it on the opioids that called out her name when she tried to stop using them. I blamed it on her past that haunts her, leaving it to haunt us. I blamed it on the hereditary darkness.

Aggressively pushing the car door open, I hurried into the driver's side of the vehicle. My eyes cast back through the rearview mirror to look at Alex. She was lying down, her eyes open with tears falling from them.

"Hey, don't cry. It's going to be okay," I assured, even though I felt like crying myself.

"Mum is not a bad person. I know that she isn't. If I ever die, I just want to make sure you don't forget about her. Continue to help her as if I were still alive," Alex let out as I started the car. My eyes narrowed as I processed her words.

"You are not *dying*, so don't say anything like that again. You are going to help me get Mum sober. I know that I can't do something like that without you, okay?" I reprimanded her. We were already down the road, I was driving at the speed limit—possibly a little faster than legally accepted.

She didn't respond to my words, so I took it as her agreement. When I looked through the rearview mirror once more, I could still see the tears in her eyes.

"You're not dying."

ANASTASIA

eukemia. My little sister had stage four leukemia. No matter how hard my mind tried to grasp that there was almost nothing the doctors could do, I failed.

I stared at my sister, who was sleeping soundly due to the medicine the doctor had given her. I couldn't help but pace back and forth around the room as I tried calling my mother over and over again. At first, it seemed as if she were ignoring my calls, but it soon turned into every call I made going to voicemail.

Throwing myself on the chair, I brought my hands up to my face as tears streamed down my face. I could only focus on the dust that fluttered around the room as I thought about not being able to see my sister again. Never in my life could I imagine having to bury my little sister. She was always supposed to outlive me.

A knock sounded on the door, leaving me with a mere moment to wipe my tears away before it opened. A woman strolled in wearing a smile on her face. I knew she could see how I had just been crying because pity began prancing around all over her face, but I didn't need any of her pity, I just needed Alex to be okay.

"I'm sorry, but I must say, you might need some sort of help. Going through this is a very scary process, and I'd hate for you to do this all on your own," the lady said. Based on the pantsuit instead of scrubs or lab coat, I could tell she wasn't a doctor.

My shoulders dropped as I turned toward Alex. "I'm fine because I'm not alone. I have my little sister right there. She's helping me by staying alive—that's enough for the both of us," I stated. The woman gave me one more smile, with pity dancing around on the rim of her lips, before glancing down at her clipboard.

"I wanted to stop by and explain what leukemia is and what to expect throughout this entire process. As mentioned, Alexandria is suffering from stage four leukemia. Most cancers are staged based on tumors and the amount of spreading. Leukemia is based on blood cell counts and the accumulation of the leukemia cells in organs. Alexandria has a very rare case for her age of chronic lymphocytic leukemia. It has spread to her liver, her bone marrow, her lymph nodes, and her blood. It's spreading through her body like a wildfire," the woman explained. As she talked, I could just feel my hands shaking, and my mind screaming at me. I am such a terrible sister. How could I have not known my sister was sick all this time?

"The doctor can't state how long she's had the disease, but he says that it doesn't look good. We can get her started on chemotherapy as soon as possible to see if we can kill any of those cancerous cells and relieve some of her symptoms. A really good doctor who wants to help Alexandria is arriving soon. He is on his way and will do his best to assure a potential recovery for her," the lady finished, allowing faith to surge into my heart. As scary as my sister's cancer sounded, I only hoped the doctor was as good as the lady said he was.

Taking a deep breath, I tried not to cry in front of her. All I could do was nod my head while she began to write some more things down on her clipboard. The sound of her pen scribbling down nonsense flowed into my ears.

"I'll let the doctor know to get her started on chemotherapy right away. Now, we have to discuss the ugly part of this. Do you happen to have insurance—Medicaid, Medicare, anything to help cover expenses?" the lady asked, raising a brow as she sent a soft, reassuring smile my way. I bit down on my lip as I shook my head. *They're asking for some way to pay for all of this.* My head began to spin as I thought about the cost of everything. I thought I was in debt already seeing as my family was behind in almost every bill, but now, with Alex's medical expenses, we would be completely robbed of money for years. *Maybe I could pick some hours up at the diner, or I could even find a second job.*

"We can't deny you care, Ms. Smith. No matter what, we'll be sure to do all we can for your sister, but the cost will pile up quickly. Cancer treatment isn't cheap," she said softly.

Closing my eyes, I could feel a stray tear roll down my cheek. Before it could completely fall, I harshly wiped it away.

"Okay," I whispered.

Her features slowly returned to a soft smile as she wrote more things down on the clipboard. "I'll be back shortly after discussing future treatment with your doctor and seeing what we can do to help you out financially."

The moment she was gone, I picked up my phone and dialed my mother's number. Once again, it went straight to voicemail. As soon as I hung up the phone, a sob ripped out of me.

"I hate her! I hate her so fucking much! Why can't she just be a normal parent for once?" I shouted.

When I turned to glance at my sister, she was already staring up at me. A look of melancholy was obvious on her features. After closing my eyes and taking a deep breath, I smiled at her. "How do you feel?"

"Nana, I know she isn't the best Mum in the world. We live in a world that wants to bring us down. We waste so much time being angry with others and ourselves. *I'm still here, aren't I*? I'm still breathing, and I can still move." She chuckled before raising her arms up and down. "Hate is an ugly word. Mum is still in there somewhere, and it is nothing but a waste of time to hate the disease that is keeping her away from herself. Time is limited in this world, and if we don't look for the positive moments—what the hell are we living for? You're my big sister, and I'll love you always, no matter what you do with your life. I may be dying of a disease, the same way she is, you need to stick by her exactly like I know you're sticking by me. We need to—*ow*."

I gasped out as she gripped her side with a grimace on her face. Instinctively, I reached out for her, hoping she would allow me to be there for her.

Suddenly, her eyes widened as she looked up at me. "How are we going to pay for this? Mum can't work with the record she has, and you can't afford this treatment," Alex pointed out.

"Don't worry about anything. I'll figure it all out, like I always do. I'm going to go call a nurse," I said, touching the top of her head before walking out of the room. One of the nurses automatically perked up from behind the desk. She walked around the counter to come toward me.

"She keeps clutching her side in pain," I informed her. She quickly nodded before entering the room. Her eyes were immediately on Alex as she began to do something with her IV.

"I'll be right back with some more pain medication. Dr. Flores is one of the best oncologists in the nation. He is eager to meet you, Alexandria. He'll be here as soon as he lands," the nurse stated with a bright smile. Once she finished changing the IV, the nurse exited the room.

"Don't you have to work today?" my sister asked.

One thing I love about Alex was her intelligence. I knew that when she spaced out, it was her intellect putting things together. Her mind had a way of solving the impossible equations of life.

"I'm chucking a sickie," I told her. She looked up at me, then rolled her eyes playfully. The longer I looked at her, the more I didn't want to ever leave her side. What hurt the most was realizing that my sister may be dying. *No, she's going to live no matter the cost—I will do anything to make sure she is okay.*

Her eyebrows rose as she looked at me. I quickly averted my eyes and picked up my phone. Alex hated signs of pity almost as much as I did. Not many people in the world can say that they like to be looked at with sympathy when they were struggling. For me, it was like someone was rubbing it in my face—that there was a thick wall blocking me from a solution.

"Mum isn't answering," I said, setting my phone down on the hospital's bedside table.

"Go, swing by the house and check on her. I don't trust that man we saw her with," Alex replied, a frown on her lips.

The nurse walked back in and handed Alex some pills and water. Heading out of the room, the nurse gave me a small smile.

My sister already looked comfortable and ready to fall right back to sleep as she rolled over onto her side.

"I don't want to leave you here by yourself. What if your

doctor gets here?" I asked, grabbing a hold of her hand. From her words about not trusting the man, worry began to knot in the pit of my stomach.

"Nana, my sunflower…I promise you I am going to be okay. I'm already," she yawned, "so tired. Go check on Mum. The nurses will watch me, and I'll make sure we don't start anything without you."

"Okay, but I'll be right back," I declared. She waved her hand dismissively as she shut her eyes. The medicine they gave her seemed to work pretty quickly; she was out in seconds.

I decided to watch over her for another minute and then grabbed the keys. I left her room and wandered down the stairs to the entrance. As I made my way outside, I walked toward my car, staring at my reflection through the window. My hair was a mess and I was still wearing pajamas. The sudden cancer wasn't anything I could've prepared myself for. Everything went south within a minute.

As I opened the door, I carefully slid into the vehicle before turning on the ignition.

* * *

"MUM!" I shouted out as I walked into our small apartment. All the lights were off, but it was only because our electricity still wasn't working.

Stepping one foot into the house, I grabbed the gun by the door. There was also a flashlight we kept inside of a drawer that I hurriedly reached for. We were an apartment full of *only* females, aside from that, my mother tended to bring men around like it was nothing. We had all agreed that it would be smart to keep a gun around just in case we needed it to protect ourselves.

One small step after another led me straight to my mother's room. I knocked softly, and when I didn't hear any response—I went in. Grabbing better hold of the flashlight, I flicked it on.

A gasp moved past my lips as I ran over to my mother who was passed out on the floor. Her room was a mess and there seemed to have been blood dripping from her nose.

"Oh, my god! Can you hear me?" I shouted, grabbing her face gently. Her mouth moved to form a groan as she nodded her head. I didn't know what to do.

"Yes, yes, I can hear you," she whispered. Leaning up, a groan left her lips as her eyes remained shut. Shaking my head, I grabbed my mum and pulled her onto the bed.

It quickly became our normal routine: help her remove her shoes, lay her down on the bed, place the blanket over her body, and leave. Only this time, her room looked like it had been trashed, and she looked like she had been trashed right along with it.

"What did he do to you?" I asked as I began to remove the heels from her feet.

The temperature in the apartment made it challenging to even think straight.

"Who, Dante? Oh, no, nothing, sweetie. He just gets a little rough. I'm sorry I couldn't get the money this time," she slurred. I went up to her and tucked her into bed. She was quivering, making me quickly realize she was high. There was never a time that she wasn't drugged.

"What did you take?" I asked, my voice going robotic.

"Nothing, sweetie. I didn't take anything…how's my little girl doing, is Alex okay?" she wondered. It sounded like there was actual concern in her voice, but I knew she wouldn't remember any of this. So, I settled with a sigh as I ran my hands through her hair. Her body kept shivering as I did so.

"She has cancer, Mum," I said, a tear falling from my eyes. Mum looked up at me, her eyes were so bloodshot and empty. I had to fight the urge to slap her and scream about how she needed to be there for us. She needed to know that it's her fault I will never be financially stable because the car, apartment, utility bills, and hospital information were all in *my* name—they're always going to be left unpaid. I wanted to scream that I can't handle all of this on my own. I needed her to understand that my little sister was necessary for me to be *sane* because there was no one else in the world who cared for me as much as my little sister did, not even my own mother.

"I can't blame you, because then I'd have to blame it on your mother, your mother's mother, her mother's mother, and so on. I'd have to blame it on the darkness. Mum, I don't blame you, but please," I sobbed as she began to fall asleep in my arms. *Please just love us more than those damn drugs.*

ANASTASIA

I fell asleep in a hard chair right beside Alex's hospital bed. With a groan, I lifted my head from the palm of my hand as my eyes began to adjust to the light. I could hear my little sister's voice, but it was just taking my brain a while to process her words.

"Okay, that sounds terrifying," Alex said. With those words, I immediately snapped out of whatever trance I was in before I looked up at my sister. Her head angled toward me as she shot me a gentle smile. I couldn't help but notice her cracked lips and the alarming paleness of her skin.

"Morning, my little emoji. The doctor is finally here," Alex said. She had a great way of not showing how much pain she was in. If someone random were to walk in, they never would've been able to guess that her organs were dying.

"How do you come up with yellow things like that on the spot?" I asked, chuckling softly. My hands rose to my face just to make sure there was no drool on the side of my mouth as I tried my best to fix my hair. Then, I finally looked over at the doctor. He was a beautiful man—blue eyes, blond hair, white teeth.

"Hi, you must be Alexandria's sister. Heard you snoring a little." He chuckled, giving me a glance of those pearly whites. I smiled at him before turning toward my sister with wide eyes. She looked as if she were holding in a laugh as she watched the scene unfold.

"Yes, I'm Anastasia," I said, reaching out for a handshake. It had taken a while for me to grasp the American custom of a handshake. I wasn't used to that sort of thing in Australia.

"Anastasia. That's a beautiful name. I'm Dr. Jacob Flores, your sister's oncologist," he said, looking into my eyes for a moment. Suddenly, Alex cleared her throat, leaving me to narrow my eyes at her.

"I was looking at her scans and her body is equivalent to that of a sixty-year-old woman's," he began.

"Okay, *ouch*. Just rip the Band-Aid off, why don't 'cha?" Alex sarcastically exclaimed. A small chuckle escaped from me as he sent her an apologetic smile.

"When they handed me the scans, I would have never been able to guess that she was a seventeen-year-old girl. The cancer shouldn't be attacking her organs so aggressively. I thought about removing the cancerous organs with a transplant, but that takes months. Months that she may not have," he said.

My eyebrows pulled together as I processed his words. "Months that she may not have? What are you saying?" I asked, my hand instinctively reaching out for my sister's. He had a sad look on his face, a look that was full of pain and sorrow. The only look in the world that I did not want to see coming from a doctor.

"Look—"

"How many months do you think she has?" I asked. He

glanced down at Alex, who sported wide eyes and parted lips as she looked at him.

"Maybe we should go out—"

"How many months?" I demanded.

He let out a sigh before walking toward me. "Luckily, the cancer hasn't spread to her kidneys. Once it does, I'm predicting based on the way it's aggressively attacking her body and the amount of chemo she's going to go through—I believe that she has two months. If we would have caught the cancer sooner, she would have had a better fighting chance. I'm sorry, but I'm afraid it's too late," he said, his voice dulling in defeat.

My shoulders fell. I wanted to scream and cry, but I knew that I couldn't do that in front of Alex. I had to be strong for my little sister. It wouldn't be fair for me to break down. When my eyes met her coppery gaze, I had expected them to be full of tears. They weren't full of anything. It had to be her overachieving mind attempting to find an answer to all of this.

"I'm sorry, but we are going to do the best we can to make sure that the cancer does not spread. There have been many patients that we predicted would survive for only four weeks and ended up living for ten years. We never truly know, we can only predict. Your sister is in the best hands possible, and I'm going to make sure that we give her the longest life we can," he promised.

I hated how I couldn't form words. I wanted to be able to say all the right things to make everyone feel better. The truth was it was always Alex who did that. I was the negative one, but Alex always remained hopeful.

The doctor's eyes yearned for me to trust him. They were begging me to relieve my worries by having faith in the professionals. Little did he know, bad luck was common in our family. The second we open our hearts to having faith or putting trust in someone, we would end up being reminded of why that voice in the back of our head screamed at us not to.

"Thanks," I gritted out, my voice shaking. I wasn't sure what I was thanking him for, but the word flew out of me because it was the only word that didn't sting.

"I want this to be easier for you, I really do. Trust me when I say that I'm giving this one hundred and ten percent, Ms. Smith," he pleaded. He gave me one last look of sorrow and then proceeded to walk over to Alex. "I'll see about starting you on that chemotherapy in about thirty minutes."

After she nodded her head, the doctor turned on his heels and walked out of the room. I watched his retreating figure before my eyes shut tightly.

"You have work in an hour. You should go home and get ready," Alex stated calmly, as if her oncologist hadn't just told her that her world could possibly end within two months. It left me puzzled. How could she do such a good job at feeling so unbothered?

"Alex—"

She raised a hand, stopping my words. A frown coaxed my lips at the sight of her shaking her head back and forth. "No, my little taxicab, I don't want to hear it. He said there is a chance I could live beyond that. I've always been a fighter. So, I'm going to need you to go to work, be normal, and just try not to worry so much about me. I'm okay," she affirmed.

"I wish you would stop comparing my hair to yellow things," I said, a chuckle escaping me to make up for the amount of sadness I was currently feeling. She smiled at me, beaming happily. Another thing that I loved about her was how happiness radiated off of her so effortlessly. I didn't know what I would ever do without that.

"What's the fun in that?" she asked, quirking up an eyebrow. It felt odd how she decided to avoid everything the doctor had said. I wasn't sure if she was covering her disappointment with humor, or if it was because she truly felt hopeful.

"I wouldn't go to work if I didn't have to come up with some way to pay the electricity bill. It doesn't feel right to be working, leaving you in here all by yourself," I told her, running my hand through her hair.

"I promise that I'm okay. Please, just go to work," she told me. I sent a forced smile her way before going over to grab my bag. I quickly shoved my phone inside of it. As I walked away from her and toward the door, I could feel something trying to drag me back. I wasn't sure if it was guilt or if it was my overprotectiveness urging me to stay.

Just as I was about to turn around, Alex yelled out, "Leave!"

Smiling to myself, I walked out of the room. The doctor was standing behind the counter, conversing with the nurse, before his eyes caught mine. I wasn't sure what they were talking about, but it didn't look like it was good.

As I stood there, the oncologist made his way over to me. He was wearing a kind smile, but there was something in his eyes that didn't quite match.

"Ms. Smith, are you heading out?" he asked.

"Yeah, I don't want to, but I have to go to work," I told him, narrowing my eyes. "Is there something you need to tell me?"

He sighed. "Her cancer has spread more quickly than we thought. She was having pains in her side yesterday. So while you were sleeping, we did a couple more scans of her body. The cancer has now also spread to her kidneys."

"I have to go to work," I whispered before walking past him and out of the hospital. There was a burning sensation lodged in my throat that spread to my heart. I didn't want to lose Alex. I couldn't be alive without her!

I quickly made my way to my car just as tears began to pour out of my eyes. My sight was so blurry from crying that it made it almost impossible to unlock the door. As frustration burst through me, I kicked the side of the vehicle as a sob ripped out of me.

"Ms. Smith!" the doctor called out. Turning toward him, I quickly wiped my tears away. I made sure to rid any evidence of my sorrow because I needed to be strong.

"It's not safe for you to deal with all this stress by yourself. I've seen her records, I know that you're only twenty years old, taking care of a seventeen-year-old teenager with cancer. It's okay to see someone or lean on a friend in times like this. I've seen what this has done to families, I can't imagine it for one person," he advised.

"I appreciate your concern," I told him, smiling sadly and successfully unlocking my door. After quickly pulling the car door open, I sat down in the seat, leaving him standing right beside my car. With the key in the ignition, I started it up. As he still stood there, I decided to roll down my window.

"You have a strong kick there, by the way. You know, I may not be an orthopedic, but I'd be more than willing to check your foot out if you need me to," he told me, offering a kind smile.

"I'll keep that in mind," I chuckled unenthusiastically. "Goodbye!"

* * *

"Girl, what's got you so bummed out?" My co-worker, Liliana, had asked me while I was placing burgers on a tray. She stood right by me with her hand on her hip as she awaited my answer.

"My sister is probably dying of cancer, and I have to sit here and pretend that everything is okay. I just can't stop thinking about her," I answered honestly. She reached out and touched my shoulder. A small smile made its way onto her features. I looked over at her dark complexion and big bouncy curls that fell down her back. Liliana was a beautiful girl inside and out.

"My mom passed away from lung cancer when I was younger. She always told me to stay strong, so now I am telling you...stay strong, Anastasia," she said, opening her arms. I walked into them, allowing her to hug me. Her hug was soothing me, calming me in every place my crying heart hadn't stop its weeping. It felt like the hug a mother would give their daughter, but she was my twenty-year-old friend who could make me feel more at home than my *actual* home.

"I don't even know how I am going to pay for everything," I whispered.

She pulled away from the hug quickly before pointing toward a table of people in suits. "Okay, this is going to sound really crazy, but we should switch tables. That man over there," she said, pointing toward a handsome man with loads of tattoos. One tattoo in particular that stuck out like a green thumb was the huge angel on his neck. "His name is Vincenzo Rossi. He has a half-brother who owns this huge underground club. My cousin works there and she just bought herself a mansion."

"What could she possibly be doing at a club to make that much money?" I questioned.

"She strips, okay? It isn't as bad as you think. If it wasn't for how overprotective she is, I would've been stripping my way into Italian pockets as well. From what she tells me, Italians love them some black girl magic." She chuckled.

"We can switch tables, but I'm not sure if I'm going to strip," I told her, grabbing the tray she had already prepared for them. Nodding her head, she grabbed the burgers I prepared, heading over to my previous table.

Taking a deep breath, I walked over to the huge group of men. The second I made it in front of them, I could feel all of their eyes on me. Setting the food down on the table, I tried to pretend as if I didn't feel all of them looking me over.

"Is there anything else I could get you guys?" I asked, my voice soft and full of nervousness.

"Anastasia," one of the men had read my nametag out loud as he looked at my body. Tucking a loose strand of hair behind my ear, I nodded while waiting patiently.

"Has anyone ever told you that you resemble a Barbie doll?" a different man asked.

"Leave it to you to play with dolls," Vincenzo growled out in —what I would later come to find out as—Italian, irritation visible in his words before glancing down at his phone. I wish I understood what he was saying, but I knew no other language than English.

"Valentino Romano would love you. Valerio, leave his card for the girl," the first man said. All of the men seemed to chuckle darkly. A rush of gratitude flowed through me. I didn't have to do much to get offered the job, and it was almost like fate planted it in my lap. Finally, they grabbed their food and walked off.

When I glanced down at the table, there was a huge tip and a card with the words 'Valentino Romano' written on them. Biting down on my lip, I thought back to my sister. Without a second thought, I slipped the card into my apron. I'd do anything for Alex, even if that meant stripping.

ANASTASIA

$\mathcal{I}$ sat in my car with my eyes gazing down at the business card in my hands. My previous conversation with Liliana kept playing over and over again in my head. *Stripping?*

I didn't know the first thing about stripping, but then my thoughts traveled over to my sister. Deep down, I knew that if I could make as much money as Liliana's cousin does, then maybe I could also help my mother as well. All she needed was some mental help. Maybe with the right amount of extra money, I could provide that for her.

Taking a deep breath, I grabbed my phone from my pocket before typing the numbers on the card. Each number seemed to make my heart thump a little faster. Finally, I pressed the little green button signaling to call.

"How may I help you?" a lady asked over the phone. Her voice wasn't exactly as welcoming as I expected it would be. It seemed as though she were in a rush and the last thing she wanted was to be on the phone with some wannabe stripper.

"Hi, my name's Anastasia. I was curious about employment," I said, cringing. I sounded so awkward.

"Anastasia, hm? What are you, Australian, British?" she asked with a hint of curiosity. I didn't even need to see her face for my nerves to flare up. Perspiration began coating my face and neck.

"Australian," I muttered.

Annoyance settled in my gut. I hated how intimidated I was over absolutely nothing. It was very unlike me.

"Let me guess, you came here to America thinking it was the land of opportunity only to find out that it isn't. Now, you have no money and no other choice but to strip or whore around, whatever the hell floats your boat, am I close?"

"Not even. I'm only calling because I need a job. I didn't ask for your assumption of my backstory!" I snapped.

"Hmm, so you do have a little fire. I'm only a bartender, but how about I put you down for an interview tomorrow at noon? Since I like you, I'm going to offer you a little piece of advice—wear sexy lingerie under your clothes. Also, make sure you at least know the basics. See ya," the lady said unenthusiastically before the call disconnected.

I stared down at the phone in my hands with wide eyes. That went a lot better than I had thought it would.

As I sat there in the parking lot, I turned on a video to show the introduction of stripping. Just as I was beginning to get settled, a knock echoed through my car from the window.

I looked over to see Liliana, who was looking at me as if I had just grown a second head. "Girl, what the hell are you still doing here?"

Finally, her eyes settled on the video playing out in my lap. When she saw the stripper showing off certain moves on my screen, realization settled on her features. I watched as she walked over to the other side of my car, where she climbed into the passenger side.

"Okay, help yourself."

When I looked over at her, she had her lip gloss out and was applying it to her full lips. As soon as she finished, she puckered her lips in the rearview mirror with a smile on her face.

I watched with a raised brow as her body turned toward me.

"Did you call?"

"Yes, I called. They said I have an interview scheduled for tomorrow. Then, the girl went on to say that I should wear sexy lingerie and know the basics of stripping. I don't know the first thing about stripping," I told her honestly.

Clicking off the video, I went on to send a text to my little sister. I didn't want to be out too late to the point that it would cause Alex to worry. Liliana only nodded her head as she continued to watch me.

Anastasia: Are you okay?

Her reply was almost immediate. I didn't even get the chance to put the phone down.

Alex: Yes, I'm fine. I'm just bored.

Alex: Actually, the nurse just came in and gave me medicine, I think I am going to go to sleep instead. I'll be asleep when you get here. Nighty, sis.

A smile made its way onto my face. My sister seemed to have that effect on almost everyone. She could make the worst person in the world smile if only she had the chance to.

Anastasia: Goodnight.

Just as I turned off my phone, I shifted over to face Liliana.

She smiled sweetly at me. "If you have time, would like to go to my cousin's place. She could teach you a few things and tell you all about the place."

I looked down at my phone once more before nodding.

Starting up my car, the music began to blast as I drove out of the employee parking lot. Liliana was singing to every song playing on the radio, no matter what genre it was.

"Where do I go?" I asked, finding an excuse to turn down the radio. I thought it would finally cause a pause in her singing, but it didn't stop her at all. All it did was make her sing slightly quieter before pointing to the left.

Following her directions, we finally made it to an enormous home resembling only something a millionaire would own. It looked so warm and nurturing due to the woods surrounding it. I was taken aback by its enthralling beauty.

With wide eyes, I looked over at a sleeping Liliana. What surprised me was how fast she could fall asleep. She had just been telling me directions not even two minutes ago.

"Lily, wake up!" I exclaimed.

She let out a groan just before her eyes popped open. She did not look pleased. It wasn't until she sat up in the seat and looked around that realization ran across her features.

"She got this house from *just* stripping?" I asked, astonished. All Lily did was nod her head with a grin before opening up her door. I followed right behind her as I exited my vehicle.

We strolled to the house, but just before Liliana could ring the doorbell, it opened.

"Lily," a beautiful woman said, opening her arms. Liliana happily walked into them, smiling so big. It was something she couldn't stop herself from doing. Her smile was always there on her face, and it also happened to be one of the most contagious things to ever exist.

"Janice," she returned the greeting.

Finally, they pulled apart and Janice smiled at me happily. She was slightly taller than average height, and she had a body to kill for. Just like Liliana, full lips sat perfectly on her face.

"Is this the friend you told me about? Anastasia, isn't it?" she asked, raising a perfect brow at me. Nodding, I watched as she tied her long, beautiful curls up into a bun, making sure to tuck a loose strand behind her ear. She nodded toward the inside of her house before backing away from the door.

"Nice to meet you," I said, extending an arm for a handshake. She completely ignored my outstretched hand and went straight for a hug.

"These Italians wouldn't be able to keep their hands and eyes off of you! You're gorgeous, has an accent, and a nice body. Plus, you're a natural blonde. We don't have anyone like you at the club. The men there seem to love anything exotic and erotic," she said, smirking as if a plan was forming in her mind.

"Come, let's teach you how to be irresistible!" She smirked before grabbing my hand and dragging me toward a room.

The moment we were inside, I noticed how it was just a dim room with a stripping pole right in the middle. Chairs circled it and the thought of me being up there caused a blush to form on my cheeks.

"So, the first thing I am going to teach you is called the 'outside step,'" she said.

I turned toward her to see that she was already removing her shirt and walking right up to the pole and wrapping her hand around it. It was almost as if a switch turned on. The kind woman I had seen before quickly turned into a desirable woman.

All she did was plant her foot a centimeter away from the pole before circling her leg around it and repeating the process. She gave me a curt nod before getting off. I took that as my cue, so I repeated exactly as she did. I had to do it about five times to get the hang of it, but once I did, Liliana and Janice were both clapping their hands.

"You're a natural," Janice complimented.

A smile made its way onto my face as I got off of the pole, allowing Janice the chance to teach me something else.

"Today, I am going to teach you all the basics. We can practice every single day until you're caught up, but I think you're going to make an excellent student." She smiled.

Nodding my head, I took off my shirt and slid out of my pants, leaving me in just my unmatched bra and panty. I was ready to do this for my sister and my mother.

* * *

HOURS DRAGGED ON. Janice taught me everything I needed to know for the next day. Who would've guessed that stripping was a lot harder than it looks? Not only that, but it was also exhausting.

Now, Janice thought it would be smart to assess before calling it quits.

"Do a Pirouette!" Janice shouted out over the music. I stood on my tippy toes a couple of inches away from the pole before spinning with my hold remaining on the metal stick. Then, I leaned back against it with my foot against my knee.

Janice gave me a thumbs up with a proud smile on her face.

"A Fireman Spin!" Liliana shouted, laughing slightly. I did the outside step before clamping my knees on the pole as I dragged myself down while keeping the spin. Liliana and Janice looked at each other with a nod.

"Okay, um, do a Chair Spin," Liliana said.

I grabbed onto the pole before spinning my body around, all while sitting on air as if I were sitting on a chair. It took a lot of muscle strength. Thankfully, I had my weekly visits to the gym to keep me in shape.

"Okay, last one, do a Back Hook Spin," Janice called out. The Back Hook Spin took a lot of work, but I managed to learn it after a lot of failures. I grabbed onto the pole before spinning around and hooking my back right leg around the pole just as my body slid down, all while keeping that spin.

"Perfect! We're finished, and don't forget about the other ones you've learned today as well," Janice said just before the music cut off. I happily jumped down from the pole and put my clothes back on.

We walked out of the room and over to the dining room where there was wine already laid out for us.

I didn't want to drink since I would need to drive back to the hospital, but I still accepted my glass. "So, please inform me about this whole club thing. I saw a guy today with a lot of tattoos and he seemed scary."

"Tattoos? Were they everywhere on his skin?" Janice asked with wide eyes.

"*Yes*," I drawled out, thinking about the man. "He had this angel tattoo on his neck."

"That was Mr. Rossi. He rarely comes to the club. None of the girls have ever even seen his face, we have only heard stories about him. The man you need to look out for is Mr. Romano," she said. This only made me more suspicious.

"Okay, but why?"

"Let's just say many people compare him to the devil. If you thought Mr. Rossi was scary, wait until you meet Mr. Romano," Janice said. My eyes wandered over to Liliana to see she was passed out with her head knocked back on the chair.

"What the hell am I getting myself into?" I whispered to myself.

VALENTINO

*L*ove made people weak. Weakness was for those who loved. It was a good thing that I would never be someone like the soldier I shot. I would never sell out my business for a *woman*. Love was blocked from the stone that formed around my heart all those years ago. The only love I had were for my guns that aided me in the deaths of those who betrayed me.

My mind kept replaying the gunshots that pierced through one of Dimitri's soldiers. I never expected to obtain the expensive information that he shared with almost no problem. All I had to do was bring up the woman he loved, and he was ready to tell me everything, including something I never knew...Dimitri had a daughter. I smiled genuinely for the first time in years as I pulled back the trigger and took his life. *Dimitri had a daughter*. For once, I had the power to make Dimitri feel what I felt all those years ago.

"Valentino!" Vincenzo boomed out angrily as he stormed into my office. "What the hell are you planning?"

A small, sarcastic smile graced my lips as I held out a folder for him. It was the same folder I kept since I was nine when my parents were taken from me. The folder was only growing and growing as I found out more information about Dmitri Ivanov.

He didn't waste a moment pulling open the folder as his eyes rested on the contents. I watched as he pulled out a picture of a girl, Dmitri's daughter.

"Who is this?" he asked, placing the picture of the girl down on my desk. A smirk spread across my face as I looked at him.

"Orabella Martinez. Well, that's what she thinks. She is truly Orabella Ivanov, the daughter Dmitri loves oh so dearly and has been hiding. When we tried to take a hit out on Dmitri, we failed. He knows we're onto him, which is why he faked his death. So, now we need to turn to our plan B, Orabella. We have to move fast before he realizes we know who she is," I explained. He glared down at the photo of the girl.

"Since when do we kidnap children?" Vincenzo asked in disgust.

I scoffed. "This is an old picture; the girl is actually nineteen. Just so you can refresh your memory, Dmitri murdered our mother, who was carrying our baby sister, and *your* father. I would do anything to make Dmitri burn in all of his sins, and you should, too."

He sighed. Vincenzo knew I was right, but he was soft. His heart was too sensitive for the life we lived. He cared too much even when he tried his best to pretend he didn't. It was one of the reasons why he couldn't be Don. Instead, he became cover-up for safety purposes. Many people were more likely to fuck up in front of someone who wasn't the boss, than someone who was.

"So, what are you planning for her?" Vincenzo asked.

Leaning back in my chair, I folded my arms across my chest. There was so much brewing between me and Dmitri, I knew he was planning to attack at any moment. I didn't have enough time or energy to watch over a girl who belonged to a man I would kill with no hesitation. In all honesty, I was worried I wouldn't be as kind as Vincenzo if I met her face-to-face.

"Well, you will bring her here, watch over her until we need her, and keep her as far away from me as possible... that's all," I answered.

He rubbed the bridge of his nose as his eyes cast down at the girl. The wheels in his head were continuously turning. "Fine, but I'm only doing this for our family."

"As do I, brother...as do I." Just as my younger brother opened his mouth to speak, a soft knock sounded on the door. Vincenzo sighed before getting up from his seat and storming out of the room like a child.

I sent a small smile to Valerio, who stood outside of my doorframe, witnessing Vincenzo's child-like behavior. He was a man I trusted dearly with my club. The girls loved him and trusted him, which was essential for my business to run properly. I needed their trust.

He walked over to my desk before placing a file down in front of me. I glanced at him with a raised brow as I took in his nonchalant expression.

"What's this?" I questioned.

"A new recruit. The bartender, Kayla, told me this girl will be coming in later today for an audition, and after using her number to track this girl down, I have a good feeling about her," he informed me.

Narrowing my eyes, I gazed down at the file before looking at all its contents. Valerio always looked into potential employees' background to make sure they weren't sent from any of my enemies. Every person who walked into my club had to have no other intentions than to have a good time or to make money. It was protocol to get as much information about anyone new who entered my club.

As I looked over the file, her picture caught my attention. She looked like the kind of woman Dmitri would send to seductively get information about me. I found it difficult to believe her record was clean, but I wanted to trust Valerio's expertise in finding out everything about anyone.

"What time is she coming in for her audition?" I raised a brow.

"Noon."

"Is she a natural blonde?" I asked curiously. There was nothing more I disliked than woman who tried too hard to be something they weren't.

"I believe so, sir."

Good. She was different, and I'd be a liar to say she didn't pique my interest, which meant she would easily grasp the attention of every man in my club. With a smirk, I allowed myself to look at her one more time before handing the file back to Valerio.

"What's her name?" I asked.

He smiled gently before taking the file from my hand. "Anastasia."

ANASTASIA

"**W**here are you going?" Alex asked.

My sister had a gift for telling when someone was lying, but that didn't stop me from filling in every blank with a fib. I knew telling her the truth would tempt her to try to talk me out of it. So, with all of that in mind, I plastered on a fake smile as I leaned down to kiss her on top of her head.

"I have a job interview today," I answered.

Alex nodded her head slowly just as I was beginning to pull away. What she didn't know was that I was wearing lacy pink lingerie under my outfit. Janice had let me have it since it was too small for her, and it served as a reminder of what I would have to do.

"Why are you getting a different job? I thought you liked working at the diner. Lord knows I miss the food you always used to bring home," she said, laughing slightly. I looked down at her and tried to conceal my every emotion. As much as she tried to hide it, she looked drained.

"I want a second job," I muttered.

"What? I thought you were going to go back to school and

work on a degree. I hope you're not getting a second job because of me, Nana. I promise that as soon as I am done and out of here, I'll help pay for everything. I'm tired of you having to sacrifice so much for me and Mum," Alex said, a sternness shedding off her tone.

I was sure she didn't want me to notice how her eyelids drooped, blinking long and slow. I knew she was drifting off to sleep.

"Go to sleep, Alex. I'll be back," I told her.

She was nodding her head slowly. I gave her one last sad smile before walking out of the hospital room.

The first thing I noticed was Alexandria's oncologist. He seemed busy talking to a family, but then he momentarily made eye contact with me. It looked as though he had something to tell me, but he was forced to turn his eyes back to the couple.

Walking out of the hospital, I hurriedly made my way to my car. I didn't want him to follow me because I was too afraid of what he might tell me.

* * *

LOOKING around the dimly lit club, I quickly noticed that it wasn't packed with too many people. A girl was dancing on the pole in nothing but a pair of panties, and a few men were standing around watching her. My face flushed I was watched them, wondering if that will one day be me up there. The music was soft and the sound of glasses clinking together echoed through the room.

I turned back to the bartender. She had her black hair up in a high ponytail and lips painted in red lipstick. I could only watch as she began to walk toward me.

"Anastasia?" she questioned, a smirk lifting the side of her face as she gave my body a once-over. I watched as she nodded her head in acceptance of my physical appearance.

"I'm assuming you're the woman I spoke to on the phone," I replied.

"Yes, the name's Kayla. Walk with me, I'll be taking you to the employment director," she declared. Kayla didn't even provide me with the chance to say anything as she turned around and began to walk me backstage. I hurried behind her, just before the automatic door could close. The hallways seemed to last forever. It took a good couple of minutes before we finally made it to a door. She twisted the door-knob and opened it up.

"Valerio, it's that new girl we were talking about," Kayla said.

I stepped into the room to see a man with chestnut blond hair. The room was empty for the most part. A stripper pole was centered in the middle of the room with a few seats and couches surrounding it. I was sure the room was used for parties. I glanced up toward the stripper pole. My heart sank at the realization that I was actually going to do this.

"Okay, Kayla, you may leave," he urged her.

She sent a small smile my way, whispering lightly, "*Good luck.*" I gazed at her until the door shut, leaving us inside of a room all by ourselves.

"Your name is Anastasia, correct?" he asked. I could hear the slightest Italian accent in his voice. I wondered if he was the Romano guy everyone was talking about.

"Anastasia Smith." I grinned.

He smiled slightly, nodding his head as he looked down at my body. His eyes settled on mine once again. It was the look he gave me—almost as if a lightbulb flicked on in his head the more he looked at what I've to offer. For some strange reason, I was not as nervous as I thought I should be.

"My name is Valerio Vitali, the girls all call me V.V. Now,

this interview is more like an audition. It isn't going to be something you may be used to, and if at any point you feel uncomfortable, please be sure to let me know," he kindly replied.

Nodding my head, I felt relief flow through me.

"I am going to have to ask you, do you have any experience in pole dancing?" he quizzed.

"No, I've only worked as a waitress in a diner."

My heart pumped in my chest as he examined me. I wondered if he could see through me right to my thoughts. What if someone saw me out there on stage, what would they think about me? Would they think I was some disgusting girl who lacked intellect, that the only good thing about me was my body? Would my sister see me and shake her head in disappointment? Was I just Mum—*a disappointment*?

My shoulders tensed up and my heart began to hammer in my chest. I wasn't sure if I could do it anymore. There was this urge to hurry and leave, but I kept thinking about my sister in the hospital. She needed me, and I didn't want to fail her.

"Perfect. Let me tell you something, dancing is the body's way of releasing emotions without words. It is neither dirty nor scary, *but* it is beautiful. So, I am going to dim the lights a little and play some soft music. All I want is for you to convince me with your body that *you*, Anastasia, are *beautiful*," he affirmed. The tension in my shoulders began to ease as I took a deep breath. I removed the t-shirt I was wearing as slowly as possible. My goal was to be seductive, but I was sure that awkwardness coated my every action. Hairs on my body stood at attention, even my mind was racing off in every direction. I was nervous, and I was sure that Valerio could feel it.

"Eye contact. Eye contact shows confidence, as if you own

what you are doing," Valerio suggested. My eyes reluctantly met his, where I could see the interest lurking behind them. While never looking away, I slid my shorts down my legs and let them pool at my feet.

He smiled proudly as I anxiously walked up to the pole. My back was turned toward him at first, but I quickly grabbed onto the pole and tossed my head back to look at him. I did every move Janice taught me, including a freestyle of my own. The more I danced, the easier it became. I found confidence cheering me on and loved it profoundly.

When I finished, he was clapping his hands. I watched him as he got up from the couch and walked toward me.

"I love this pink on you," he said thoughtfully. "As you were dancing, I was thinking about something that will especially set you apart from the rest of the girls. The pink, blonde hair, blue eyes—the thought of a Barbie doll comes to me."

"As long as I get the job, I don't mind being Barbie." I chuckled.

"You've convinced me—you have it. Let's talk about money. Most of our women here rack up on tips, and we men have money to spend. You also get paid twenty dollars an hour. If you keep practicing, based on the way you look on that pole, you could end up walking out of here with no less than a grand a night. Since you are only beginning, I'm going to start you out at six o'clock in the evening to two o'clock in the morning on Saturdays and Thursdays. If the men here want to see more of you, I will simply add more days," Valerio explained.

I nodded my head with a smile. I never even made close to a thousand per check from the diner, and he was saying that I could end up with no less than that per day. It was way more promising of a deal than my other job.

"Great. It was really nice meeting you, Anastasia. When

you arrive on Saturday, just go up to Kayla and she will get you started," he added.

I looked down at his outstretched hand before giving it a firm shake. After a curt nod, he exited the room, leaving me by myself. As soon as the coast was clear, I let out a loud squeal as I picked up my clothes and began to redress myself.

ANASTASIA

The smell of booze and sweat infiltrated my nose as I walked around the club. Even though I should have been anxious, I couldn't help the swarm of happiness in my heart. Alex was doing a lot better. Her treatment was really helping with not allowing the cancer to spread further. It always made my day to hear Dr. Flores talk about how well she was doing. Since Alex was getting healthier, I truly began to worry about her finding about my secret job.

Janice was still giving me lessons every day. Sore muscles and bruises pinched my skin, and I still had trouble getting up on some mornings.

Despite all good things, I still hadn't heard from my mother in a long time, but everything else was really starting to look up. It was finally Saturday, and that meant I would be working as a stripper for the first time in my life.

There were a lot more people than there were during my interview. Men in suits were everywhere. They were speaking a foreign language, downing drinks, laughing. Women perched themselves on poles while others swayed their hips as they pranced.

"Anastasia! Come, you have the next dance. I will show you where to set up," Kayla said, appearing out of nowhere.

I followed her into a back room where a few women were putting on makeup. There were about fifty vanity mirrors. All of them had curling irons, straightening irons, and makeup.

"This one is yours," Kayla told me before pointing toward an empty space. It had pink plastic lingerie with knee-high boots to match. On the clothing, there was a sticky note that read '*Barbie*' in cursive print. There were even specific directions written on it. They wanted my hair to be tightly curled, my makeup to be a simple pink lipstick, winged-eyeliner, and pink eyeshadow.

"Be ready in thirty, Barbie." She winked.

Once Kayla exited, my eyes wandered to one of the girls. She was dressed as a leopard. Her nipples were covered by a piece of tape, and her panties were a simple thong with a tail hanging from it. She must have felt my eyes because she looked over at me.

"What? Do you have a staring problem?" she snarled.

Rolling my eyes, I turned back to my reflection. Thirty minutes wasn't long at all, so I quickly turned on the curling iron and began to curl my hair.

When I finished with everything else, I threw on the pink plastic clothing. The bra lifted my breasts a lot, making them look bigger and perkier than they actually were. Even my panties hid themselves in my butt. Then, I slid on the boots. The heels were about five inches tall, and they made noise with each step.

"Barbie, really? How pathetic." The leopard girl chuckled as the girl next to her began to laugh. It was quite ironic, seeing as she was dressed as a leopard.

"Oh, shut the hell up," Janice said, walking into the room.

The leopard girl narrowed her eyes at me before facing herself in the mirror.

"You're on. Remember what we rehearsed," she whispered in my ear before giving me a small wink. I took a deep breath as nervousness spread through me.

As we walked out of the room, I couldn't ignore the whisper I heard, "You said Mr. Romano is here?"

I thought it would be impossible for my heart to thump so wildly in my chest. The man everyone was so scared of was going to be out here somewhere. I really had to do good if I wanted to keep this job.

We walked toward the back of the stage. Her hand was on my shoulder before she spun me around to look right at her. "This is why I love it when Valerio gives us a different part of ourselves. Switch off Anastasia, now you go out there to be Barbie! You're sexy, so go show them exactly what I know you can do."

The lights turned pink and music began to play. It was my cue. Pulling back the curtain, I revealed only my leg in the knee-high pink boots. I then stepped all the way out with the beat of the music. I bit down on my finger before I trailed it between my breasts, then lower, to the waistband of my panties. Men began to shout in appreciation as I pulled the hem of my plastic thong low enough to almost catch a small glimpse of my womanhood.

Leisurely, I strolled toward the pole. Just like Valerio had told me, I made eye contact. What I didn't expect was to make it with one who sat back in his chair dangerously. His hair was slicked back and his eyes were focused on me. He had to be the most beautiful man I had ever seen. If it weren't for the flashing red lights and the nonexistent, yet huge *beware* sign on his forehead, I might've actually been tempted to get his number.

I grabbed a hold of the pole and did a pirouette that

caused the men to throw money. Only then did my body swing around the pole before I stayed in the air, revealing almost all of myself as my legs split into a V-shape. The shouts began to get louder once I spun around and down the pole until my legs froze in the splits.

Once again, my sight fell on the man. He was wearing a smirk on his face. My body moved of its own accord toward the edge of the stage. Men were quick to slide money into my boots, my bra, and my panties just so they could cop a feel.

Finally, the music ended. I walked off the stage, hearing the foreign cheers of all the men. Just as I was about to head off to find Janice, my wrist was grabbed. A gasp fell from my lips when I quickly noticed it was the man I had seen while I was dancing. Not only that, but the look in his eyes caused fear to strike within me.

"I want a private dance."

I got to see him up close and personal. It took my breath away how perfectly sculpted he appeared to be. "I-I don't do those."

His eyes glazed over with mischief. The man's hand never let go of my wrist. I wasn't sure what to do in this position. All that I had been taught was pole dancing. Private dancing was not in my beginner's manual.

"Ten grand," he whispered in my ear. I thought about it for a second before finally agreeing. Ten grand was a lot of money. He hand settled on my waist, walking me toward the VIP section.

Based on the way his clothes and shoes seemed to drip in riches, I could tell ten grand was nothing to him. I should've guessed that he was VIP. No one would offer a stripper ten grand just for a dance if they didn't have money to spend.

The moment we were in the red room, I closed the door behind us. There was no pole, just a couch. I could feel my heart thumping in my chest. He sat down on the couch, his intense eyes never leaving mine.

I didn't know the first thing about private dancing. The thought of running away immediately rammed into my brain as I glanced between the intimidating man and the door.

He had a smirk on his face as he watched me. I wasn't even doing anything, just standing there in a pit of my indecisiveness. He seemed to have a lot of sex appeal that piqued my interest.

"You seem nervous. Come sit," he said, patting the seat right beside him.

I looked over at the innocent cushion before walking over to sit down on it. I was so close to him that the smell of his cologne wafted into my nose. He took a long sip of the drink in his hand before reaching over and setting it down. I bit down on my lip as the music began to play in the background. He seemed quite patient.

Thinking back to the ten thousand dollars he was willing to spend, I took a deep breath and climbed on top of his lap.

The mystery man appeared shocked by my actions. I straddled his lap with my back to his front. I wasn't sure what to do next, but I let my body move against his to the sound of the music. My eyes shut as I began to get into it, my lower region rocking against him. His body was rigid and tough, I could tell he was very muscular.

It wasn't until his hand wandered to cup my bottom that I stopped. Janice had told me all about the man who owned the club. He was adamant about his women's safety.

"You're not allowed to touch me. It's against Mr. Romano's rules," I told him, my back still facing him.

"You must be new. What's your name?" He chuckled. His voice was so sexy, it made my thighs clench together.

The man grabbed my hips before turning me to face him

as his eyes settled on my breasts. Slowly, his eyes wandered back over to my face.

"Anastasia. Who are you?" I asked.

The way my heartbeat seemed to accelerate did not go unnoticed. It might've been because as my eyes searched his, I couldn't see anything but emptiness and lust.

"Mr. Romano. Now," he paused, searching my eyes for some response. Fear flooded my body as he stated his name, and I was sure he could see it. "Open your legs."

My breathing quickened, and I didn't know whether to defy him or not. "I'm not a prostitute. I just dance, okay?"

He licked his lips again with a smirk that never faltered. Slowly, he lowered me onto the couch. My bareback hit the cushioned seats as my wet pussy never broke contact with the middle of his slacks.

"I just want to welcome you, Anastasia," he said, burying his face into the crook of my neck. My eyes shut at the sensations I was feeling. He was unintentionally grinding into me and everything just felt so right.

"You welcome everyone this way?" I whispered. He chuckled slightly, his lips lightly grazing my neck.

"Just you. I promise," he responded.

When his hand gripped the hem of my panties, I wanted to explode from the sensations. Desire was clouding my brain with every movement he was making. I wasn't sure what was so intoxicating about this man, but I knew that I couldn't get enough.

He pushed my panties off to the side, where they stopped just where my boots began. My breathing was too heavy to even allow any thoughts.

I looked down, preparing for him to stop, but when his eyes met mine—I knew I wanted it. He locked me in a trance with the way he peered at me. A shudder ran through my body when his finger lightly grazed my wet lips. As he entered me, I wiggled against his hand, moaning. He then added another long finger in between my walls, and it really had me screaming out. I was humping against him, dying for more friction.

Finally, I closed my eyes because I couldn't take it anymore. He was diving into me, kissing, sucking at my neck. When he began to rub my clit, I lost it. My head was tossing back in excitement to accommodate the strokes of his fingers.

"Oh, shit," I moaned out.

Soon, I shook hard and lost myself in the intense sexual satisfaction he was giving me. He hardened his grip on my thighs and explored deep into me with generous finger strokes.

"Oh!" I gasped as my hand found his thick hair. My legs wrapped around his head, making sure I kept it in place. With both his fingers, it didn't take long for me to come.

When I looked up at him, he placed the digit he had fingered me with inside of his mouth. Everything he did was absolutely sexy. I quickly pulled away and got up from the couch.

My mind was bouncing off the walls. I didn't know what to do. He was just staring at me without saying any words. I made sure to stand in the corner of the room, making sure I was as far away from him as I could be.

"Valentino," he said.

My eyebrows came together as I looked at him. He smirked in response before getting up and walking toward me. His hand landed on my hip as his head buried itself into my neck. I was pressed against the wall with his erection pressing into my stomach.

"I want you to call me by my name. Valentino," he said.

My eyes shut as he gripped my neck and turned it in the

opposite direction of his face. A whimper climbed out of me when he pressed me harder against the wall.

"Fine," I whispered.

His lips grazed my jawline and I wanted to melt. The second he let go of my neck, I turned to look at him right in his eyes. There was so much desire swimming around it was terrifying me. When my eyes wandered down to his lips, I quickly looked away.

"Until next time, Barbie," he stated.

When he let go of me, I felt like I could finally breathe. Then, he walked out of the room, leaving me in there all alone. I quickly swallowed the air I had been holding as I tried to organize my thoughts.

He was the man everyone was so afraid of, but Valentino didn't seem like the worst person in the world. He appeared more dangerous than scary. I opened the door and exited, only to be met with the loud music of the club. I quickly made my way toward the back when I was pulled by someone.

"Where the hell did you go?" Janice asked, her eyebrows pulled together, worry drawn all over her face.

I bit down on my lip before looking around in search of Mr. Romano. He was nowhere to be seen. It was almost as if after our little heated session, he had disappeared.

"If I tell you, you have to promise not to judge me," I tell her.

Her eyebrows were still raised as she awaited my answer. I grabbed onto her arm and took her somewhere more private.

"You know Mr. Romano, right?" I asked.

Her entire face dropped as she nodded her head slowly. "The man I told you to keep away from because he lives a very dangerous lifestyle?"

"*Yes,*" I drawled out guiltily.

"Gosh, Anastasia! What did you do?" she questioned.

My shoulders dropped in defeat. I hated that I let him do what he did, but I didn't hate how pleased he made me feel. It made my body ache for more, but I knew that I couldn't let that happen.

"I didn't know who he was at first. When he asked for a private dance, I was going to let him down. Then, he offered me ten thousand dollars so I said yes because I really need the money," I explained calmly.

"You gave him a dance? That's fine. It is honestly kind of shocking, though, he never asks for dances. He checks out the club for a second and then leaves," she informed me.

"That's not all," I whispered.

Her mouth dropped. For a second, I thought she was frozen. Janice wouldn't even blink, and it was starting to scare me.

"I promised Liliana that I would take good care of you. You do realize that you are on Mr. Romano's radar now. What he chooses to do with you is out of my control. He's a lot more dangerous than you think," she proclaimed. It was hilarious how scared she looked for me. He seemed like a harmless man. Maybe everyone was just overreacting.

"How dangerous of a lifestyle could he be in? It's not like he's in the mafia or something." I laughed. I saw that she was not laughing with me. Her face was as hard as stone. "He is, isn't he?"

She let out a sigh before nodding her head. My face immediately dropped. All I felt was fear strike itself into my heart as I thought back to what happened.

"So, this club is, what? His way of laundering dirty money? Now that I think about it, all of these men are mafia men, aren't they? That's why they always wear the damn suits!" I exclaimed in absolute horror. Everything was beginning to click into place as the wheels in my head turned.

"I'm sorry I didn't tell you."

"Janice, what the hell did you get me into? I didn't sign up to be working as some mafia stripper," I told her. The danger I could put myself in didn't even play as a factor in my mind. I only worried about my sister. I didn't want her to be put in any danger.

"Look, it isn't as bad or scary as you think. Valerio is in the mafia and he wasn't a bad guy at all, right? It's just Mr. Romano and Mr. Rossi that any of us girls worry about. Everyone else is absolutely harmless," she said like it was absolutely nothing.

Shaking my head, I walked away. I wasn't upset with her, I was upset with myself. I should've listened to Janice when she told me about Mr. Romano. Something about him was just pulling me in and it was impossible to stop it.

I spent the next couple of hours trying to get the entire situation out of my mind. I mingled with a few girls and even got to be a waitress. Luckily for me, there were no more men asking for private dances with an offering of ten thousand dollars.

As soon as my shift was over, I made my way backstage, where I grabbed my phone, my keys, and everything else I had brought before changing back into my regular clothes.

I completely forgot to say goodbye to Janice as I exited the club and headed over to my car.

The moment I started up my vehicle, I could feel a set of eyes burning into me. I looked up and my eyes caught those familiar sets of blue ones. It was Valentino himself, leaning against the wall with a cigar in his mouth.

I licked my bottom lip as I stared at him before starting up my car and driving away from the club. I was going to stay away from him, he was a risk I wasn't willing to take.

For my family, the last thing I could afford were anymore risks.

ANASTASIA

"Today marks two months and she's only been progressing, Ms. Smith," Dr. Flores started with a smile gracing his features. I couldn't help but cheer in happiness as I ran over to hug my sister. Her color was already returning, she was no longer as pale as before.

"Does this mean she can come home soon?" I questioned.

His smile dropped slightly as he shook his head. "Alex is progressing, but we still have to keep her close in order to monitor her. If things keep going how they are and if the chemotherapy continues to destroy more cancer cells, I believe she can go home within the next week or two," he responded.

It wasn't as good of news as I had anticipated, but it was better than what could've been said.

"Hey, you're in the middle of the toughest battle, Alex. You just have to keep fighting so you can win in the end," he muttered before giving Alex a small smile. She nodded her head slowly as she puckered her lips off to the side.

"You got this," I told her.

The doctor gazed at me, but I chose to ignore him as my phone rang inside of my pocket.

"Hello?" I answered.

Dr. Flores began to explain his plan that would happen in the next couple of months with Alex. She listened sadly as he told her about her next chemotherapy treatments.

"Hey, babe. Valerio said he needs you to come down here about six. You've been requested," Janice explained.

Letting out a loud groan of aggravation, I agreed. All she did was chuckle as we said our goodbyes.

Hearing that I had been requested brought back memories of Mr. Romano. After that day, Valerio had come up to me with all the cash I made from tips and a big fat check. It was worth about twenty-five thousand and it was addressed to me from *him*. If I didn't need the money, I would've given it back and informed the man that I was not a prostitute. However, that wasn't the case because I did, in fact, need the money. I took the check and turned back on the electricity in our small apartment. I even paid the rent for the next couple of months and then put the rest into my savings.

"If your sister wants me to explain everything to her just give the nurse a call," he told Alex while walking out of the room. I pushed myself out of my thoughts before glancing over at my sister. She was looking at me suspiciously.

"What?" I quizzed.

Then, I watched as her eyes wandered down to the bag I had underneath my chair. It was the same bag I used to pack all of my clothes in just in case I had to work. My diner clothes were in there along with some makeup and a couple of Barbie outfits just so I wouldn't have to go all the way home.

"I love you, Nana, but I have noticed how you leave some nights. Of course, you are a woman, and you can do how you please, but I just—"

"You just *what*?" I asked, pulling my brows together at her momentary pause.

"I just can't help but wonder; where do you go?"

Sitting down in the chair that had become my usual home at the hospital, I thought about the answer to her words. I didn't want to lie to her, and I knew that she would use her brilliant mind to put everything together eventually. However, her disappointment was just something I couldn't handle.

"My second job. Stop worrying so much about me, you should be the main focus," I told her, wanting to drop the entire subject.

She opened her mouth as if she wanted to say something else, but then she closed it. A sigh moved past her lips as she let her shoulders fall in defeat.

Dancing at the club had gotten easier, and the men began to know my name and they loved me. It seemed like every day that I went, the more money in tips I seemed to make. I had already bought my sister a few wigs that were waiting for her inside of our room for the day she comes home. I even updated her entire wardrobe after paying off a few of her medical bills. Life was beginning to look up for me.

"I'm going to swing by the house to grab a few things, is there anything you need?" I asked her, standing up.

"Actually, there is something," she whispered. I furrowed my brow as I watched my sister's shaking hand rise to her head where she combed through her strands. Long pieces of hair were clinging to her fingers. My heart broke at the sight of Alex's tears as she did it again and again.

"Stop it, Alex!" I exclaimed, grabbing her wrist. As I held her wrist, I couldn't stop staring at the hair in Alex's hand. When my eyes trailed up to her head, I noticed the patches of missing hair and how thin her once thick strands had become.

"Just cut it off." Alex wept.

"What? No," I stated, releasing her wrist from my hold.

Alex glared down at her hand as she shook her head. There was this pain that arose in my throat from seeing my sister like that. I'd once seen Alex hang her shoulders in defeat. It was unlike her to be so hurt and to so easily show off that pain. She was closed off, keeping her emotions sealed.

"Then I'll do it myself," she spoke. Just as she said it, Alex reached over to her nightstand where her arts and crafts were hiding inside of a drawer. She grabbed the safety scissors, and before I was given the chance to stop her, she cut her hair.

I gasped. "Alex!"

She sobbed as she cut another chunk. I could only watch in horror as she did it again. Every time the scissors snipped, her sobs grew louder.

After one last cut, she finally stopped. Her body stilled, but her weeping grew. Alex threw her hands up in her hair as her shoulders rocked to match the music of her sadness. I hurriedly wrapped my arms around my little sister, trying to protect her from her own pain. Alex responded by allowing me to hug her and keep her protected like I always swore to do. If that meant I had to protect her from the very disease killing her, then I would.

When her crying died down, I rubbed her back soothingly. "Are you okay?"

She sniffled. "I'm fine."

"Good. Now, let's get this head as smooth as a newborn baby," I joked. Alex cracked a smile before a snort climbed out of her throat. After kissing the top of her head, I called in a nurse, who helped me cut off the rest of Alex's hair before we used hair clippers to really get it short. Once we finished, I watched Alex touch her bald head as she stared at herself in the mirror. Her wide eyes and parted lips made my frown deepen.

"How do you feel?" I asked.

"I know that I have cancer. I know that it is real and that I'm dying. This whole time it was always easy to forget about it and stay strong because my family needs me to be. *You* taught me to be, but as I look at myself with no hair," her voice cracked. "It all feels so real now. I'm *dying*, Anastasia. I have cancer."

I shook my head, tears of my own beginning to fall. "No, you aren't. I won't allow that to happen."

She didn't bother to say another word as she continued to look at her reflection. I could almost hear her thoughts, full of doubt and disbelief. There was so much I wished I could do for her, but I knew that I couldn't.

After letting out a sigh, I cracked a small smile to try and lighten up her mood. "Now that you're bald and everything, you kind of look like Vin Diesel."

"Get the hell out!" Alexandria laughed as she pointed to the door.

I couldn't help but chuckle. "What? Vin Diesel is hot!"

We continued to laugh and cry, our time together stretching into hours. I helped Alex back to her bed when the nurse came in and gave her all the medication she needed. Soon, Alexandria drifted off to sleep, allowing me to slip away.

* * *

"Mum!" I called out before flicking on the living room light. She soon walked out of her bedroom with a cigarette in her hand. Bags were visible under her eyes. I couldn't help but notice her drained expression as she stared at me. It was the first time in a while she was actually sober, and as much as I hated cigarettes, it was better than what she usually did.

"What?" she asked.

I walked toward her, only to see her eyebrows raised in question. I quickly wrapped my arms around her motherly frame and chose to ignore how her body shivered even though the room was not cold at all.

"Are you okay?" I asked. "I came to tell you that Alex has progres—"

"Anastasia, do you think I could borrow some money? I promise I will give it back. I just need a little to tide me over for a little," she cut me off.

My eyebrows scrunched together. "Tide you over for what? I bought food for you, I paid all of the utility bills, and the rent. What could you possibly need money for?"

She looked away from me, preparing to share another lie. A dangerous fire was settling in my bones as I waited.

When I walked in to see her sober, a feeling of hope surged through my body. I wanted to talk to her like how we used to talk all of the time in Australia. She used to be such a great mother before she met her friend's *disappointment* and *drugs* after bringing us to America. She promised us a better life, but so far, it only seemed worse. I would have gladly accepted the cruel man that my mum once called her husband, who beat on her more times than I could count than having lost my mother in a battle of sobriety. I could never understand how that same man was the father to a kind girl like Alex. Luckily, she doesn't remember a single thing about him.

It would've been great to have someone who understood how I felt about Alexandria's situation, but instead, I was faced with a mother who only wanted money from me. Even though I have had to deal with this for so long, it always managed to sting.

"You know," she began. "Girl products."

I rolled my eyes before grabbing my bag and walking right past her. When I opened our bedroom door, I immediately wanted to scream. All of the clothes and shoes I had bought for Alex were gone. It didn't take a genius to know who took them. I threw my bag on the ground before sitting on the bed with my hands in my hair.

"Fuck! Fuck! Fuck!" I yelled.

Tears no longer threatened to fall from my eyes. All I could pinpoint was a feeling of numbness that traveled from my thoughts to my heart. There was so much stress in working two jobs, taking care of my little sister who was battling the deadliest thing on Earth, and having to watch over a mother who no longer felt like being a mother at all.

"Fuck," I whispered

I placed clothes and shoes into my bag. Irritation was clear in my expression. I was angrier with myself; I should have known she would do something so selfish. I needed to learn to be more careful with what I left in my mother's care.

Grabbing my phone, I sent a quick text to Alex, informing her that I would be heading off to work.

The stare of my mother's eyes, burning at me from the entrance of my bedroom didn't go unnoticed.

"Don't you ever ask me for a penny of my money! You should be ashamed of yourself! You sold all of the things I bought for your very sick daughter," I snapped, my eyes never going to meet her.

"I didn't do that! Anastasia, baby, you know I would never," she lied, walking toward me. I grabbed my bag and stormed out of the room. Nothing will ever make up for the wrongs she had done.

Just before I walked out of the house, I snatched off the necklace she had gotten me many years ago, it was a locket of me and a woman I once loved to call my mother.

Gripping her hand, I placed the necklace in her palm. "That is all you will receive from me ever again Sell it, trade it, shove it up your ass for all I care."

Without another word, I walked out and made sure to slam the door behind me.

* * *

I STROLLED INTO THE CLUB, only to be immediately met with Valerio. Relief quickly washed over his features as he grabbed a hold of my arm. I thought he was going to push me to the back, but instead, he walked me up the stairs. As we walked, my eyes wandered down to my attire. I was in a pink leather skirt, a white crop, and clear heels. I was nowhere near prepared for where he was taking me.

The second he opened the door, my eyes widened as I looked around. It looked like I had just stepped into a mansion. Everything was huge and dripped with expense. Even the smell was rich and elegant. I looked at Valerio.

"I am so confused. The club is a part of a mansion?" I asked.

"Yes, the club is underground. This mansion is a private home to Mr. Romano and Mr. Rossi. As for why you get to see it, Mr. Romano has requested your presence. I'm not sure what for, but I am aware of a meeting he's having," Valerio explained. My eyebrows were still bunched up as we continued to walk. The place was heavily guarded with tall men, ready to pounce on whoever necessary.

We made our way past the kitchen, where a blonde-haired lady was cooking. Her eyes met mine and I saw pity swim in them.

Past the kitchen I saw a staircase as we strolled by. I then eyed Valerio as he knocked on a wooden door. I was still confused as to why my heart began to beat wildly in my chest. I was going to see Mr. Romano again after that strange night at the club.

"Come in," a cool voice stated.

Based on the chill that ran through my body, I knew exactly who it was, Mr. Romano. Valerio opened the door, leaving me to gaze into the room. All I could see were men in suits and some women sitting beside them who looked quite bored.

There was an empty seat between Mr. Romano and a man who looked kind of similar. Only this guy had a bunch of tattoos covering every bit of his skin. Janice had told me about Mr. Romano, but I began to wonder if he was the other man Janice told me about, Mr. Rossi.

Everyone turned to look at me while Mr. Romano leaned back in his chair with a smirk on his face. "Sit."

Looking around the room, I slowly made my way over to the seat. The man covered in tattoos looked quite annoyed.

"As I was saying before the interruption," Mr. Rossi said, glancing at Mr. Romano.

I failed to pay attention as Mr. Rossi talked. They were speaking about matters that I had no clue about, or the will to learn.

Suddenly, I could feel a hand on my thigh.

My gaze traveled up to meet Mr. Romano's. Shaking my head, I grasped his hand and pried it off my thigh.

I had made a promise to myself to stay away from him. Janice warned me of his kind of business, and the last thing I wanted was to get my family into any more drama.

When his hand went back to my thigh, he squeezed it tightly before traveling up. My breathing was beginning to increase dramatically when his hand reached inside of my skirt.

"There is a reason why we have invited all of your women here today," Mr. Romano said, causing me to listen and stare right at his perfectly sculpted face. From his plump lips to his jawline, even his piercing shed with danger. As I looked at his eyes, I could see the secrets begging to be heard.

"Well, everyone except my brother," he said, causing a light chuckle to settle around the table. I looked over at Mr. Rossi to see his eyes narrowed into little slits as anger oozed from them. I never would have guessed that they were brothers. They could have been like Alex and I, only half-siblings, seeing as their last names weren't even the same.

"Many have considered me to be cruel and heartless, yet my *friend* here..." he began before beckoning for one of the suited men to stand. The man quickly stood up on wobbly feet while fixing his suit in the process. "...is getting married. His wedding ceremony will not only be paid for by me, *his friend*, but he says that I get to invite the people of my choosing as well. Isn't that right, Marco?" he asked.

I could hear the evil intent in his voice. It was enough to make my eyes narrow in suspicion as I saw Marco visibly gulp. I felt bad for him, and I wasn't even sure why yet.

"Yes, sir. Thank you, sir," he sputtered out quickly before sitting down next to a woman, his fiancée. She immediately wrapped her hand around his arm as she gazed at Mr. Romano with fear-laced eyes.

All of a sudden, Mr. Romano's hand found the outside of my panties and he brushed against my core. I immediately grabbed his arm to halt his actions, and thankfully he did stop. However, he didn't pull his hand away.

"Next time I hear of a marriage, it better come from you. This is my kindness to you, Marco, because I would gladly kill your fiancée right in front of you. You really thought you could just hide this engagement from me? Get married right underneath my nose? No. Any woman that you allow into this business should be run by me. I must know everything from the last whore that you sleep with to your preferable brand of fucking toothpaste. Do you understand me?" Mr. Romano asked, anger slipping through his words. I flinched as he slammed his fist down onto the table. "That goes for all of you at this table."

If I thought I was confused before, I was beyond confused now. His words began to process in my mind as I started to get fearful. *Did he really mean he would kill someone's fiancée just for failing to bring it to his attention?* A shiver ran through my body as I gawked at him.

"That is all I had to say. You are all excused," Mr. Romano said.

Everyone quickly fled the room, except for his brother, who moved at a slower pace. Mr. Rossi's eyes fell on me as he stared at his brother while shaking his head. There were no more words exchanged before he walked out of the room, leaving us all alone.

I got up from the chair, but his hand on my thigh stopped me. "You stay."

My heart was pumping vigorously in my chest. I kept repeating the promise I had made to myself in my head over and over. His eyes were staring into mine and it made me wonder how someone could look so perfect.

"I am not your puppy that you can call on whenever you want to. Secondly, I don't even understand why I was brought here," I pointed out.

Mr. Romano was known as a man without mercy. What I expected as a response was anger, but instead, he smirked at me. Not knowing whether to be scared or grateful, my eyebrow rose in question.

Abruptly, he leaned in closer, his lips freezing me in my spot as they grazed against my jawline. I was hoping he didn't notice the shiver that flowed through me.

"You're right, you're not my puppy. You're my little Barbie doll, no? I get to play with you when and how I want," he whispered into my ear as the hand he left perched on my thigh began to move against my clit. "As for the other thing, I wanted to let you know of your invitation to my friend's wedding. No need to be rude to me, Barbie. I only want to be your friend."

I grabbed his hand, and with as much strength as I could muster, I pushed it away from my thigh. The sound of my underwear snapping back into place didn't go unnoticed as he chuckled darkly.

"I saw and heard what you do to your friends, that is the last thing I want to be," I said behind narrowed eyes. Even though I sounded confident, my heart was pumping with fear. I knew what his hands were capable of, and for some reason, my body wouldn't run the hell out of the room.

"What do you want to be then?" he asked with a smirk still playing on his lips. I felt his other hand easily make its way up from my waist and toward my breast. As I began to let go of his hand that was prepared to finger me, I reached for his other hand. It was becoming a game of *'Don't let the mafia man grab your body parts.'*

"I want to go back in the club and make as much money as I can," I stated. Like before, I tried to get up but he grabbed me and dragged me onto his lap. I couldn't deny how aroused I was beginning to feel by being on top of him. Who was I kidding? A single glance in my direction had me wet.

"I pay you for your company," he explained, as if that was supposed to make me feel better.

"What kind of person do you think I am, your escort?" I challenged. He shook his head, his hands wrapping around my waist, pulling me closer to his chest. I could smell his rich cologne but couldn't exactly pinpoint what kind it was. Based on how much money he seemed to have, I was sure that it could've been custom made.

"Do you want to be?" he asked. I grabbed his hands on my

waist before dropping them to his sides. Getting off his lap, I turned around. The moment I did, he pushed me down so my chest laid on top of the table while his hands moved down to my bottom.

"I was kidding. Why don't you let me joke?" he asked, pressing his hard-on against me. I bit down on my lip as I could feel every inch of him upon me. All I could hope for was that he wouldn't lift up my skirt to see how wet he made me.

My mind was too busy with an internal battle, so I didn't pay much attention to his hand trailing underneath my skirt. Instinctively, I pushed closer against him, leaving his hand that was once underneath my skirt to come crawling up to my neck.

"What do you want from me, Mr. Romano?" I seethed. His hand wandered down from my neck to my waist, where he pulled up the tight fabric of my crop top. The feel of his skin against mine only built the sensations deep within. My eyes shut momentarily at the thought of everything he could do to me.

"Valentino," he said. I had to stop myself from moaning when his hand disappeared into my crop top and pushed past my bra. His flesh was against my bare boob with his erection pressing right up against my most sacred area. Biting down on my lip, he teased the bud of my nipple, leaving me to warn my hip not to make any movement against his.

"I want to fuck you right on top of this table," he muttered. A small squeal escaped my mouth when he flipped me over so my back was pressed against the table. My eyes met his darker ones. Desire was pooling in his eyes as he looked at my body hungrily. It was as if he hadn't eaten in months and I was his first meal.

. . .

I SHOULDN'T DO IT. My family would be in jeopardy and Janice warned me that he was a man to not be played with. However, one thing I couldn't deny was how turned on he made me. My breathing was growing heavier by the second. Without another thought, I grabbed him by his neck and pressed his lips down against mine. He immediately dove his tongue into my mouth, exploring everything I had to offer.

My legs immediately wrapped around him as I pressed against him. Slowly, my body began to move against his as his mouth wandered lower to my neck. A moan ripped out of me as his hand cupped my tit before his mouth returned to mine.

I ignored his fingers that unwrapped my legs from around him right before he pushed my skirt down my legs. The feeling of being completely bare except for the panties I had underneath made everything feel even better. His hand moved my panty aside like he had done previously while his mouth had never left mine.

My back arched, leaving my breast to meet his chest once his finger had dived into my sex. I broke the kiss once again when a moan shredded out of me. I felt on fire as he pulled away to look at me. He bit down on his lip while his finger pummeled in and out of me at an inhuman pace. When he added a second finger, it took everything for my body to not cave into my desires.

If I thought my breathing was heavy before, I was not prepared for how hard I was breathing now. The eye contact he held with me was almost promising. It was as if he were telling me that he could do so much more with me, and that it was a guarantee I would feel blissful no matter what it was.

Not much time passed before I could feel my lower region tightening against his fingers. It happened before I could stop it as an orgasm washed through me. I let out moan after moan until I was finished.

He removed his fingers from inside of me with a smirk. Then, he brought it up to my lips with a knowing look on his features. "Taste yourself."

I looked down at his fingers to see my juices had coated them. Staring intensely into his eyes, I stuck my tongue out. His eyes dropped from mine to stare directly at my lips right before placing his fingers directly on my tongue. I grabbed onto his hand so he wouldn't pull away and gently wrapped my lips around his fingers. He looked hypnotized when I sucked them and swirled my tongue against the tips of them.

"*Cazzo, mia bella*," he said softly before sitting down in his chair directly in front of me. I quickly sat up on the table, allowing my eyes to drop down to his erection. He was extremely hard and it looked like it would tear me apart. My eyes picked up on how it was straining against his slacks.

"You never truly answered my questions," I muttered softly.

He gazed at me for a while, then pulled me right back down onto his lap. I allowed him to grab a fistful of my hair before his head buried itself into the crook of my neck. The feeling of him sucking against my skin caused me to try to push him away, although, no matter how hard I pushed, he pulled me even closer.

"Mr. Romano, you're going to leave a hickey and I still have to work tomorrow," I groaned irritably as he continued to suck against my skin. Attempting to push him away again didn't work, but he did stop momentarily before moving on to somewhere else.

"Mr. Romano," I repeated.

His hand latched onto my waist where he squeezed me. While his one hand held onto my waist, his other one was still gently pulling my hair to keep me in place. Despite the fact that I just had an orgasm, he was making me feel turned on once again. Every time he sucked against my skin, I felt a jolt go directly to my core.

Seeing as he held on to my hair, I ran my fingers through his. I never would've guessed his hair would feel so silky and thick. When I grabbed a handful and tugged it gently, he let out a small groan against my neck. It was the sexiest noise I had ever heard. He pressed me closer against his erection and just like I had done before, I began to grind against him.

After much time, he pulled away from my neck. I just knew that it looked bad based on the smirk he wore on his face as he stared at it. "Every time you strip, I just want those little boys to know that you belong to me, *no*?"

"I don't belong to you," I said before quickly getting out of his grip. I bent over as fast as I could to grasp my skirt that he had discarded on the floor. His eyes followed my every move as I quickly slid it back on.

Annoyance was clear on my expression. I hated how much of an effect he had on me. One minute I was ready to submit to him and do what he wanted because my brain was clogged up with lust. Then the next, a reminder of the type of business he does would go rushing into my head. I had to get away, but no matter how hard I tried, my body wouldn't let me.

My phone rang, interrupting my thoughts. I quickly grabbed it and felt my heart sink at the realization that it was coming from the hospital. He got up from his chair and made his way over to me, where he pulled me against him.

"Ms. Smith? We need you at the hospital as soon as you can. The doctor received an urgent call from your sister's room and we've tried to reach you for a couple of hours. They are currently rushing her to surgery," she explained. My heart immediately sank at her words. I couldn't even form a sentence as the repetition of everything she had to say kept playing in my brain.

"I'll be right there," I muttered before hanging up.

It had been two months since Alex had been diagnosed with leukemia. I couldn't ignore the fear that crept up my bones at the thought of her possibly dying. Mr. Romano pulled away from me as he looked at my face. I quickly wiped away a tear that had fallen before briskly walking over to the door.

"I have to go," I whispered. My voice wasn't trustworthy at all, so a whisper was all that came out.

As fast as I could, I opened the door and walked out of the huge mansion and back into the club. Valerio cast me a concerned look.

I knew I couldn't handle bringing up my situation, so I just left. I left the club, I left my boss, and I left Valerio. A sob climbed out of my throat as I tried my best to breathe. It seemed like one thing kept tearing me down after another. As soon as I took one step forward, I was pulled ten steps back.

I RUSHED INTO THE HOSPITAL. My makeup probably looked a mess and I knew that my clothing wasn't the most presentable. None of it mattered though, I just needed my little sister to be okay. She was my last little bit of sanity that I had left, I didn't know what I would do without her.

Just as soon as I walked in, Dr. Flores came up to me with a tight-lipped smile. It wasn't his usual smile where he proudly displayed his pearly whites, which left me worried.

"Anastasia, I'm happy to inform you that Alexandria is in much better condition. I had to perform a splenectomy, which is surgery to remove the entire spleen. It was an emergency operation because her spleen had been dangerously compromised by the leukemia. The spleen is a very important part of the body's immune system. Seeing as we had to remove that, it's going to lead to a lot scarier bumps up ahead. This is what I call the 'dark part' of cancer, Ms. Smith. Remember when I told you that you may need help? This is the time that you should get it," he said, his hand rubbing my shoulder soothingly.

I understood that it was supposed to be good news, but I couldn't stop my tears. I wrapped my arms around him and sobbed. It may have been inappropriate to hug my sister's doctor, but it was the one thing I needed at the moment—a hug. My body shook and there was an ache beginning to make a permanent home in the pit of my belly.

"She's not going to get better, is she? She's never coming back home," I cried as I pulled away. His eyes strayed away for a moment before returning back to mine with a sad smile.

"It depends on the way her cancer responds to the treatment."

VALENTINO

I watched her run out in a frenzy. At first, I believed she was a spy or someone trying to bring me down, so I ordered my men to watch her. It was the only explanation I could think of without raising the suspicious brows of my men. She came out of nowhere and was exactly what I favored in a girl. It was easy for me to assume one of my many enemies assigned her a job to get information about me, but I was wrong.

What my men reported back surprised me. She spent nights at the hospital, watching over her dying little sister. There was no indication that she was in contact with Dmitri or anyone else who could possibly want to bring me down. My paranoia quickly vanished the moment I began to discover more about her.

What began as a task to see if she was who she truly said she was became a worry of whether or not everything was okay. I knew how easy it was to be tempted by darkness in dark times, but she was too bright of a person. It would pain me to see the same darkness in me exist in her.

What intrigued me most about the girl was the way she

would spend hours and hours at the club, just to spend all of the money she made on her sister. In a way, she reminded me a lot of myself. Maybe that was why I couldn't rid myself of the thought of her.

Vincenzo walked into the conference room with a raised brow. I rolled my eyes, not wanting to hear him go on and on about Anastasia. She was neither his concern, nor would she ever be.

"You brought one of your whores to a meeting? What the hell are you doing?" he questioned.

"She's not my whore. The girl just needs…" I trailed off.. I knew what I was going to say before I stopped myself. I was going to say that she needed someone, just like I wished I had someone. The world was lonely when there was no one there, and based on the shakiness of her voice earlier, I wasn't too sure her sister would be around for much longer.

"I thought you promised to never let those girls into our home," Vincenzo said in disbelief.

I sighed. "She's an exception. So, accept it and leave it the hell alone."

He didn't seem pleased with my answer, but he dropped it. Instead, he began telling me more information about Dmitri. Dmitri was planning something huge, and I knew it was coming straight for us. He knew we had his daughter, and it was only a matter of time before he tried to come and get her. All I knew was that we had to attack before he could get the chance.

"About Orabella…" Vincenzo began.

I cocked a brow as I gave him a pointed look. The last thing I wanted to talk about was that girl. It wouldn't surprise me if she were just like her foolish father. She probably believed the world belonged to her, and she would take down anyone who disagreed. Just like her father did to my family.

"She isn't bad. I know because I've talked to her. She seems so upset and lost. I just can't understand how she is such an angel yet her father—"

"Killed our family! Don't you ever fucking forget it, Enzo, do you understand me?" I yelled.

With a clenched jaw, he nodded. I didn't mean to let my anger take control, but I couldn't hold it back. I didn't care if the girl was nice or cruel, she was a pawn in the plan to take down her father. There was nothing more or less to the story. She was the spawn of someone I hated, which made her someone I loathed.

ANASTASIA

I woke up with a crick in my neck. I wasn't exactly sure how long I could continue sleeping on a chair. It was becoming the most uncomfortable place, but I still managed to make it work with a hospital blanket draped over me.

The second the sunlight fanned my face, I opened my eyes to look at my sister. She was still sleeping, and the slight amount of color that had managed to make its way onto her face seemed to have disappeared. Her body looked lifeless with the amounts of tubes and added monitors attached to her body.

She seemed to feel me looking at her because her eyes snapped open, but then shut due to the sunlight. When a groan moved past her lips, I knew my best option was to cover up the windows with the curtains.

"Hey," she said softly.

Her voice no longer sounded the same. I tried my best not to break down and cry because it seemed like I had done enough of that to last a lifetime. I gazed down into her eyes only to see they looked defeated. The color that once danced around her hazel gaze seemed to vanish. I was looking into them only to see myself looking back.

"Here, drink some water," I whispered before grabbing the cup the hospital had provided and placing the straw against her lips. I waited until she finished to set the drink down on the small bedside table.

"How are you feeling?" I questioned. A weak smile formed on her face before it fell. Her eyes shut momentarily as her body seemed to adjust to long, abnormal blinks.

"I'm so tired, Nana," she whispered. Her eyes shut completely, and my heart began to break. I got down onto my knees beside her bed and reached for her hand.

"Just rest a little, okay? I'll be right here, Alex. I'm so sorry for not being there when you were hurt last night. I thought you were getting better." Frustration at my doings were looming into my emotions due to my constant crying. Crying never fixed anything.

"Not that kind of tired. I'm tired of feeling like this. I feel deader when they try to cure the disease than when they just leave it alone. I'm tired of fighting. I want to be there for you and Mum, but I can't do this anymore," her voice cracked. I watched as the tears sparkled between her closed eyelids. My own tears began falling threatening to fall as I pressed her hand against my head.

"Don't say that, do you hear me? You can't, Alex. I need you! If I could, I would trade places with you in a heartbeat, you know that, right?" I sobbed. She opened her eyes before swallowing. Alex shook her head back and forth.

"It seems like I won again because I would do the same for you, which is why I am the one lying here right now. Anastasia, you have always been so capable of being a person the world should look up to. I look up to you, and I hope that one day someone will see how great of a person you are. I hope that *you* will see what a great person you are. I love you so much, and no matter what happens, promise me that you will love yourself just as much," she stated.

Something felt like it was squeezing my heart. I couldn't believe what she was saying, and I didn't know how to feel. Was it selfish of me to beg her to continue to fight despite the fact that it was *killing* her, or was it selfish of her to give up on me?

"It doesn't matter because I will have you to remind me. Alex, please, you have to stop talking like this. It's been two months and you made it past what everyone said you would. You can do this, I know you can! You're my little sister, but you're the strongest person I have ever met," I pleaded. My hand went up to touch her cheek. Her body was cold and drained as her eyes stared into mine. Slowly, she brought her hand up to lay on top of mine before giving another weak smile.

"I will do my best for you. It's the least I could do, seeing as you have taken such good care of me. I promise I will fight, but if anything happens to me, I just want you to take care of Mum. I want you to remember everything that we've ever talked about. Live on my legacy of forgiveness and love." She chuckled softly. I sniffed a little before responding with a light chuckle.

Reaching over to the bedside table, I grabbed the water and pressed it to her lips.

"Nana, if you give me any more water, I am going to become Aquaman in this bitch," she joked. It caused me to laugh even with tears falling from my face. Only she could do that for me—make me laugh while I was crying my heart out.

"I love you, baby sister," I muttered before pressing a kiss on top of her head. She smiled at me before puckering her lips and kissing the air. "I love you too."

The door opened and Dr. Flores walked in wearing a huge smile on his face. "Alexandria, you're up!"

She grimaced at the name he called her. No matter how many times she tried to get him to call her 'Alex,' he always managed to call her by her full name instead. I sent him a small smile.

Last night after the hug, we had a long conversation where he told me about the death of his father from cancer. Apparently, he lost him when he was really young, which was what made him want to be an oncologist. The story was a saddening thing to hear, but he managed to make it sound motivational.

He returned the smile before looking over Alex's vitals. Once he finished, he held his fist up to her as if she were a five-year-old. Tiredly, she gave him a fist bump before lowering her hand back down onto the bed.

"How are you feeling?" he questioned. I looked over at her. Her answer to me replayed itself in my mind. She gave him a small smile, her lips were cracked with dryness as a tint of blue made their way onto them.

"Like a million bucks," she muttered with a light chuckle. He smiled but it didn't reach his eyes.

"Very funny. Really, how are you feeling? On a scale of one to ten, can you state the amount of pain you are in?" he questioned. My eyes dropped down to her, only to see the smile she had on her face had disappeared.

"Ten," she whispered, a tear rolling down her cheek. It broke me to hear that, and based on the glance that the doctor had given me—he could see it on my face. Instead of dwelling in sadness like me, he gave her a small smile before nodding his head.

"Okay, I'll get the nurse to bring you some more pain medication. Hang in there," he told her. Using his fingers, he signaled for me to walk outside the room with him. I hugged myself as I accompanied him just before sparing one last look at Alex to see that her eyes were shutting.

"She looks so weak," I announced sadly the minute we had exited the room.

"All of the chemo, the surgery, and the radiation are beginning to really take a toll on her body," he explained. I couldn't help but frown at his words. My eyes wandered over to my little sister through the small window on the door.

"It's true, isn't it? That the treatment for cancer feels worse than the cancer itself?" I asked, even though I already knew the answer. For some reason, I couldn't tear my eyes off of the beautiful young girl who seemed wiser than us all.

"Yes, that can be true," he answered.

"The treatment isn't even going to take the cancer away. It has spread too much to the point of no return. You're only prolonging her life now, am I right?" I asked, trying to hold back the tears. It felt like something was clawing on the inside of my throat just trying to get out.

"Anastasia, what she needs right now is someone who believes in her. Just stick by her side and help her fight this cancer as much as you can. I know it must suck hearing this from me, but she's channeling your strength. I still remember the day she told me that you were the person she looked up to because you stayed so strong for everyone else. Stay strong," he told me. I quickly wiped away a stray tear before nodding my head at his words. I still felt like I was drowning, trying to get to the surface, but no matter how many times I tried, I couldn't. There were no words I could say that would make anything better.

"The nurse will arrive shortly with her medicine." He nodded just before walking off. I turned back into the room and sunk down on the chair. It sucked that I didn't need a mirror to know that I had bags under my eyes, and they were bloodshot. All I could do was stare at her and keep watching her heart monitor.

"Stop looking at that thing, sis." She chuckled. I smiled down at her before nodding. The doctor said I needed to be strong, so that was exactly what I planned to do.

"The pain medicine should be arriving any minute now," I told her, followed by a wink.

"I know you think I call you yellow things because of your blonde hair, Nana. That's not it at all. I call you yellow objects to remind you of your spirit. Your spirit is so *yellow*, it's like the light at the end of the tunnel. You give hope, and you attract the darkness by turning them into their best possible selves. You are so yellow—full of intellect, beauty, and positivity. Thank you for everything you've ever done for me. Thank you for being like the sun after rain, the way it beams on every piece of land— you love every part of everyone just the same," she whispered.

"Stop talking like that," I reminded her. She nodded her head again without saying another word.

I just needed her heart to continue to beat. My breathing seemed to calm me by listening to hers. There was a Doyle attached to her nose that assisted with getting oxygen into her system. Every long breath that she took soothed me. Every beat of her heart calmed me. It was like I was listening to the waves of the beach while my favorite song played on a radio beside me.

Sliding the chair closer to her, I grabbed a hold of her hand. I planted about a million kisses against it.

My palm went up to her beautiful face to memorize every single detail. From the cute little nose she had to her plump lips. I even smiled a little at the scar she had on her cheek from the time we were playing hide-and-go-seek and she fell off a tree.

Before I knew it, my eyes were shutting on their own as sleep overcame me.

* * *

"GET THE CART! HURRY!" I heard someone shout. I repeatedly blinked to get the blurriness out of my eyes. When I opened my eyes to see a ton of doctors and nurses inside of the room, the confusion was clear on my expression as they rushed and ran, trying to grab supplies.

"W-what's going on?" I questioned, rubbing my eyelids with the back of my hand. My heart was pounding in my chest for some reason, and I couldn't figure out why. Slowly, my gaze traveled over to my sister's heart monitor only to see that it had stilled. My lips parted as tears filled my eyes. I could no longer hear any words. All I could see was the lifeless face of my little sister. Just moments ago, she was fine. Alex was speaking to me, telling me that she would fight for me. Now, as I looked at the line showing on her heart monitor, my world crashed right in front of me.

"Alex?" I asked, already missing the smile that would come across her face.

A nurse appeared right in front of me. She was wearing a mask to cover the bottom portion of her face, but I knew she was shouting words at me. All of her words were blocked from my eyes as my focus remained on Alexandria.

The nurse began to softly push me toward the door as I let out scream after scream, choking on my own tears. "Alexandria! Alex! Alex, wake up! Please, I need you!" I sobbed. "I'm sorry, Alex! I should have been a better sister! I shouldn't have let your cancer get so bad. I should've known you were hurting. I'll be better, Alex! I promise! Please don't leave me here! I can't be alive without you!"

The defibrillator finally began to flood my ears as

everyone moved away from her except for a doctor who held the paddles against her body. "Clear!"

"Please, ma'am, you have to leave the room," she told me. I shook my head and pushed her out of the way before sprinting over to Alex. I knew she could hear me. I knew that she would never give up on me.

"I need you! You promised you would fight, Alex! You promised! I can't do this without you, please, just wake up for me! We will take care of Mum together, and we can still grow old together! Alex! Alex, please!"

I began to shake her. Her head just rolled.

As I began to notice her lifelessness I allowed myself to get pushed out of the room. My eyes remained on her as the doctors and nurses tried to get her to wake up..

"Alex," I whispered.

* * *

HOURS PASSED. I didn't know how long I had been waiting for some sort of news. I found myself staring off into space with thoughts of never being able to hold her again. My hands were remembering every trace of her skin. I could still feel her cold hand in mine. Visions of the times we laughed and played kept going on in my mind like a movie I wished to see for the first time again.

I felt a hand touch my shoulder. When I quickly turned around, my heart broke into a million pieces. Dr. Flores was no longer smiling. He didn't have a single bit of hope anywhere on his face like he usually did. There wasn't even a tight-lipped smile. For as long as I've known Dr. Flores, I had never seen a tear in his eye, until now.

"I'm sorry—"

"No! No! She's not! *She's not*! I know Alex. She—she wouldn't leave me! You didn't try hard enough! She's not *dead!*" I shouted. Tears clouded my vision. Shaking my head back and forth, I kept telling myself it was some sick joke. Alex told him to lie and say she's dead just so she can laugh because Alex always had this strange dark humor.

"Anastasia, Alexandria didn't make it—"

"No!" I sobbed.

My body shook and I could feel my veins being pulled from my body. Somebody was suffocating me with sorrow and no one in the world was helping me stop them. The world got rid of the wrong person by choosing the best one. From the way Alex smiled to the way she always held our mother every single night before she went to bed. Alex never cared that our mother didn't want us, she always saw the good in her. She always saw something that I could never see. She saw the yellow in me while my heart had always felt colorless.

"Why would someone so pure be taken away from me? She never did anything to hurt anyone. She always wanted the best for every single person in the goddamn world! My little sister made me feel like a child with the way she could uplift the spirits of those who were hurt!" I cried.

Dr. Flores wrapped his arms around me and let me cry out every bit of sadness. My shoulders rocked, and my head began to ache, but it was no matter for my heart. My heart hurt the worse, and the only person in the world who could fix it was gone now.

ANASTASIA

$\mathcal{I}$ shut my sister's journal and held it against my chest. It was as though I could hear her voice speaking to me as I read every word. As I read her journal, it was like we were having conversations again. My heart ached to hear her voice, listen to her laugh, and voice her beliefs. Alex had always been there, and I felt so empty now that she wasn't holding my hand and telling me that everything would be okay. I missed her so much. If I could talk to her one last time about anything, I would. If I could look into her hazel eyes and see the gleam of hope and prosperity in them, I would.

I threw myself onto her mattress, hugging the journal as protectively as I could. Sobs ripped out of me as I called for a sister who would no longer respond to them.

I had lost her only a week ago, yet it felt like yesterday. It was the loss of my best friend, sister, and inspiration all rolled into one. I tried so hard to think of a way that could heal the open wound on my heart but only managed to come up short-handed.

The door opened, but I didn't give it any thought. I

glanced up at the intruder only to see that it was my mother. She looked down at me with a sad expression on her face then sat down beside me. I watched her as she wrapped her arms around me, leaving me to weep into her shoulder.

"I don't understand," I wailed. The journal was still plastered against my chest, which felt like the presence of my little sister. With the journal and my mother's arms wrapped around me, it made me feel whole for the first time in my life.

"I know, Anastasia. You have to take it day by day, one step at a time," she whispered before placing her lips against the top of my head.

"She was the only person in this world who believed in us, Mum. There is no happiness without Alex," I professed. I could feel her arms tighten around me, but it didn't end the feeling of loneliness that suddenly erupted through me. It only seemed to aided the thought of being all on my own.

"I'm always here," she cooed sweetly, pretending like none of her wrongful actions ever happened.

"You say that, but then you go away," I sniveled before pushing away from her as my eyes glared down into her blue ones. Her shoulders fell in defeat as she watched me. "You may be sober now, but you aren't all the time! Just tell me why you never chose us? Alex was dying and you still didn't care!"

"Damn it, Anastasia! I care, okay? I've always cared! It's hard for me to have these negative thoughts and memories all of the time. I need to let things go the best way I know how so I don't hurt you both," she explained.

"You did hurt us!" I shouted. She seemed taken aback by my outburst but understanding quickly caressed her features.

"Get out," I whispered defeatedly. My sight blurred with tears waiting to be released. I was done being disappointed by my mother. Alex may have wanted me to watch over Mum, but I couldn't do it anymore. The last thing our mother deserved was a helping hand.

"You—"

"Get the hell out of our room!" I seethed.

She spared me one last glance before getting up and walking out the door.

The minute she was gone, I opened Alex's journal back up and reread her words. The sound of her voice reading each word to me left my mind busy. I could feel the tears drop from my face, but I didn't even care to acknowledge them.

"Well, Alex," I sniffed. "I may be your yellow, but you've always been my blue. So overlooked, yet full of purity. I could picture your husband and the two—no, *three* kids you would have. You would even have a dog named Spot that you'd get angry at for jumping on the couch. You've always shown the beauty in simplicity, Alexandria. My sea, my whale, my blueberry, and my butterfly—I love you, always."

After a while, my tears stopped falling. My body felt so numb and exhausted that I didn't want to move anymore. All I could do was zone out until the sun disappeared and the moonlight bounced off my body. When my gaze fell on Alexandria's mattress, for a moment, I could see her on it. *God, I miss her so much.*

Guilt coursed through me when the conversation I had with my mother abruptly made its way into my mind. Deciding to get up and apologize, I let out a loud sigh. I opened the door and walked out, making my way over to her room.

Softly, I knocked on her door but didn't hear a response. When I knocked again and still couldn't hear anything, I decided to just walk in. The room was so dark and lifeless. The smell of sweat infiltrated my nose as I turned on the life.

I should've expected it, but I decided to think she would

be more comforting. Her room was absolutely empty meaning that she had left. My mum doesn't work and she has no friends, so the only reason why she ever disappeared was to get high.

How did she get money?

My entire heart dropped down to my feet. I raced over to the kitchen where my bag sat. All of my clothes and shoes that I carried around for work were dumped out. She even took every penny I had in my wallet.

Without another thought, I began to trash the entire apartment. My brain was so clouded with rage that I gave no thought to all of the picture frames that showcased our *'happy'* family I threw on the ground. I flipped over couches, tables, and even broke glasses along with plates. Then, I walked into her room and ruined everything in sight.

Just before leaving her room, I grabbed a piece of paper and wrote *'Take that money you stole and buy new things.'*

I grabbed another bag and began to throw all of my clothes into them. Everything that belonged to me, I placed into the bag. When I finished, I left the apartment. I hurriedly ran toward my car and threw everything inside of it.

* * *

"BARBIE! What the hell are you doing here?" Janice asked in shock the minute I walked into the club. Completely ignoring her, I strolled over to the bar, where men openly bought me drinks. I ignored their thirsty eyes and flirty words as I tossed back I don't know how many drinks. Janice came up to me at some point, trying to convince me to stop drinking. The hazy state of my mind prevailed because I ultimately ended up telling her to leave me alone as I drank more and more. It wasn't until I found myself stumbling down a hall that I realized I was out of control. As I stumbled, I found myself grasping something sturdy and rigid—the wall. Then, as my hands pressed down hard, I realized it wasn't a wall; it was a muscular chest.

"Barbie?" the chest asked. I poked it and felt the smooth fabric against the pad of my finger.

"Chest?" I questioned, mocking the Italian accent.

The chest's hands moved down to cup my chin before bringing my face up to meet the familiar gaze of Mr. Romano. Then, my eyes followed his finger as he wiped some liquor off the corner of my mouth.

"Alcohol?" he questioned with a frown.

I smiled at him, showing the biggest smile I could muster. "Oops?"

He looked like some undetectable figure. As I looked into his eyes to see the sight of disappointment, my heart broke. My sister would also be disappointed in me. No matter what I did or how many shots I took, she was always there.

I don't know what compelled me to do it, but I quickly began to undo his slacks. Sadly, he immediately stopped me by grasping my hands.

"You can barely even walk. I came by and thought you were one of my whores. Do you not realize how vulnerable you look?" he asked unemotionally.

I smiled at him before leaning up to press my lips against his neck. My arms circled around him as I moved up to his jawline. Just as I was about to kiss his lips, he pushed my head away from him.

I scoffed. "So, we can only do things when you want to do them? I'm trying to give you a good time just like you do for me. I want to have sex, right here, right now."

When he didn't make a move or say a single word, I shook my head in disbelief. Slowly, I pulled away and looked into his empty eyes before turning around and walking away.

He quickly grabbed my neck and dragged me so my back was against his chest. "You want to be treated like one of my whores, hmm?"

"I want you to fuck me like one," I said seductively, a dangerous smile making its way onto my face.

Mr. Romano quickly let go of my neck and grabbed me by my arm before walking me through the entire club and up the familiar set of stairs. We made our way into the mansion where we passed many doors until he opened up one in particular.

The walls were blue and it caused my heart to still. When my hand reached over and touched the wall, it was almost like I could feel her skin. Blue, like the sea, was my baby sister.

I looked over at him and I was sure he could see just how badly I wanted to cry. However, I was glad that he didn't say anything. He only nodded over to the large, empty bed. I walked over and sank down onto the soft mattress. My heart was suddenly shattering, and I had no clue how to keep it together.

"This is one of the guest bedrooms. Go to sleep and don't leave this room until you're sober," he ordered. I opened my mouth, ready to say that I needed him to stay with me. I was fearful of my mind when I was alone, but before I could get a word in, he shut the door.

Letting out a sigh, I climbed into the bed, pulling the thick blanket over me as a frown came across my face. Just when I thought the alcohol would take its effect, it was gone.

Now I understood why my mother had taken so much money. Forgetting the pain only lasted for a few minutes.

ANASTASIA

The sunlight seeped into the room, waking me up from the deep slumber I was in. I quickly got up and shut the curtains before crawling back into bed, grumbling as I did. I wanted to be swallowed up in a pit of darkness while allowing my depressing thoughts to roam free.

It didn't seem to last long as the door opened up and a woman walked in. It was the same blonde-haired woman I had seen that one night when Mr. Romano had requested me to join him for a meeting. She smiled kindly at me before beckoning me to follow her.

"Can't I just stay in here?" I groaned.

Her features fell slightly, along with her shoulders. I noticed the way her smile was still there, but there was desperation in her eyes.

"Mr. Romano ordered me to get you something to eat. Please, come with me," she requested.

"I'm not hungry," I grumbled childishly before throwing off the blanket. I then bent down and picked up my shoes,sliding them onto my feet. "I'll just leave."

"You can leave, but maybe after breakfast. Mr. Romano

was very adamant about you coming to eat," she claimed calmly, but I caught the plea in her voice.

Letting out a sigh, I nodded my head and stood up.

We walked down the long, wide hallway up until we made it to the big kitchen. I noticed how she was already preparing something to eat on the steel stove.

"Mr. Romano mentioned you were Australian, so I wanted to make you something that could help remind you of home," she explained before sitting a plate right in front of me. The plate was filled with perfectly seasoned eggs, bacon, buttered brown toast, and a side of fruit.

"Thank you, but in Australia, all I've ever eaten was cereal, bread, and milk." I chuckled quietly. Based on the look she gave me, I could tell that it wasn't exactly the most graceful thing to say.

"Oh, no, the food looks amazing," I added, grinning.

She sent me a kind smile before beginning to clean up her mess. I almost moaned out loud from how good the food tasted. She was an amazing cook.

"It's rude of me not to know the name of the person who went out of their way to cook such a great meal for me." I smiled. I was beginning to sound like my little sister. It was quite ironic how much she seemed to rub off on me even though she was gone. The thought quickly made my smile peel off my face.

"My name is Sarah. I'm the official cook of the residence. Anytime you need me to make anything, I'll always be right here," she informed me.

My eyebrows pulled together as I took another bite of the delicious food. "So, you're telling me that you'll always be right here? Do you ever go to the restroom or to sleep?"

She laughed a little before shaking her head back and forth. "I do sleep. I'm on duty seven hours a day. Mr. Rossi or

Mr. Romano are rarely here, so I often have very long breaks," she explained.

"What are the brothers like?" I questioned.

She opened her mouth to speak, but then her eyes trained in on something behind me. I quickly turned around and caught the sight of a particular tattooed man. When I saw an angel on the man's neck, I knew exactly who it was, Mr. Rossi. His eyes were narrowed as he looked at me.

"Valentino, *since when do we allow your whores in the house?*" Mr. Rossi growled in Italian before turning around and facing Mr. Romano, who had just entered the room. Valentino's gaze traveled over to me before turning cold to look at his brother.

"Mind your business." Valentino chuckled darkly. My brows furrowed as I tried to figure out what they were talking about.

I could see the glint of mischief in Valentino's eyes as he looked over at his brother. Mr. Rossi spared me one last glance before going up the stairs, leaving me with only Sarah and Mr. Romano.

Deciding to let go of my confusion, I got up and walked over to Mr. Romano. Embarrassment was picking at my actions as I thought about what I did last night.

"Thank you for everything," I muttered, tucking a strand of hair behind my ear.

After a long while of Valentino saying absolutely nothing, I cleared my throat. "I'm going to go back to the room and freshen up, if that's okay," I muttered.

He didn't say anything, he just turned on his heel and walked away. Letting out a sigh, I ran my hand through my hair and headed back to the room.

When I walked into the guest bedroom that I occupied last night, I roamed around and opened one of the doors only to find an elegant bathroom. I stepped in and noticed the clothing on top of the counter, along with a new tooth-brush and toothpaste.

Turning on the shower, I disrobed and stepped right in.

* * *

AFTER MY SHOWER, I wrapped myself in a towel. Walking over to my reflection, I used my hand to push away some of the water droplets from the mirror. I tried to smile. It shouldn't hurt to smile, but it did.

"Nana, you know what makes me happy?" Alex asked with a smile playing on her lips. She was lying down on her bed while I was across the room on mine. I turned over to look at her and saw that she was already gawking at me.

"What?" I asked. Her gaze strayed over to look out the window, where the moon was brightening up the room, even with the dark sky trying so hard to keep the light away.

"Knowing that I have power...even if it's just the power I have over myself. That's powerful," she said, bewildered.

I thought about her words, allowing a smile to come to my face. She's right, controlling our body, emotions, actions is very powerful.

"You know what makes me happy?" I questioned. Her eyebrows rose as if she were asking me 'what?' without saying the actual words. "When you shut up and go to sleep."

She let out a loud gasp before throwing her pillow at me, laughter spilling from her lips.

I smiled at myself in the mirror again, only this time, it was genuine. It was one of my favorite memories, and it played out in my mind like it was actually happening. If I had known what Alexandria's outcome was going to be, I would have said something different. I would have crawled into bed with her and held her close to me. There was so much I wish I could change, but I knew that I would never get that time back.

When I looked in the mirror one last time, the smile was gone. There wasn't even a frown. Only a lone tear could do its best to explain everything my heart was screaming.

After letting out a deep breath, I grabbed the pink tank top with white lace dancing around the seams. After the top, I slid on a pair of shorts over my panties. My breasts were practically bulging from my top and I could make out the buds of my nipples. I was annoyed, but I loved that it was the most comfortable thing I had ever worn.

After I finished freshening up, I exited the room, making sure to shut the door behind me.

Mr. Romano was sitting on the bed. He looked hungry for something, and I had a feeling I knew exactly what he was craving.

"Mr. Romano!" I greeted, startled.

He glanced over at me before his eyes darkened as they skimmed down my body. I noticed the way he made a circular motion with his finger, beckoning me to twirl for him. Rolling my eyes, I turned around before returning back to my previous stance.

He was wearing a smirk that only grew more taunting as he walked up to me. It was challenging not to grow weak under his intense gaze.

"Do you work today?" he asked.

No words would form, so I settled with a shake of my head. What I didn't tell him was that Valerio had given me two weeks off. He didn't want me anywhere near the club while being in such a vulnerable state. I was also positive that Janice told him about my drinking episode.

"*Fun,*" he drawled out.

His arm circled around my waist as he pulled me flush against him. His body was rock hard and every bit of it was full of muscles. My eyes went up to meet him, only to see lust in the deep pools of his eyes.

"How long do you want to stay?" he asked, his face leaning down into the crook of my neck, where he already began to leave open-mouthed kisses.

My eyes shut as I bit down on my lip.

How long did I want to say?

I remembered all my clothes were locked away in my car. Not only that, but I'd moved out of my mother's apartment and was currently homeless. My plans were to ask Janice or Liliana for a place to stay for a while, but after last night, my shots at that were probably gone.

"However long you want me to," I responded seductively.

"Something is off about you," he said slowly. He was looking at me like I was a puzzle he needed to solve. The desire I had pooling between my legs slowly vanished as I wondered if he could see the sorrow brewing within me.

"What?" I asked stupidly.

He shook his head just before unwrapping his arms from around me. I thought he was about to exit the room, but he managed to take me by surprise when he settled on the bed.

My legs were rooted to the ground while I observed him taking off his suit jacket. I wasn't sure if it happened slowly, or if it was just my mind playing tricks on me. His eyes never left mine as he placed his suit jacket on top of the nightstand. Leisurely, he brought his hands over to one of the cuffs of his shirt. He unbuttoned it before rolling each long sleeve just above his elbow.

"Don't play dumb with me," he dared.

"What makes you think something is off about me?" I asked.

He chuckled darkly. I focused very closely on his hand as he easily pulled a gun from his pants before setting it right on top of his suit jacket.

I should've been more frightened that he had a gun the entire time, but at that point, I didn't care if he was going to shoot me or not. With the way my luck was, I wouldn't even be surprised.

"Normally, you'd leave while the night was young. Even on your shifts, you would leave as soon as your time was up," he pointed out. "Now, though, you stayed over last night and you still haven't raced out of here."

"You want honesty?" I questioned, waiting for the nod of suspicion he gave. "I haven't left because I have nowhere else to go."

"You don't have anywhere else to go?" he repeated.

My eyes harshly snapped over to his so he could see my irritation. "I get it. It's not your problem. I was going to ask to stay with a friend."

His perfect brow arched as he sat himself down onto the bed. With his hand, he beckoned me to come closer. I did exactly what he wanted until I was standing right in front of him.

"What friend, Bambolina?" he asked.

"A friend," I repeated.

His eyes darted down to what was right in front of his seated view—my waist. He brought his hand up to the hem of my shirt, where he fisted it before slamming me down onto his lap as hard as possible. It took me by complete surprise and left me breathing heavily.

"That was quite disrespectful," he whispered, his mouth just inches away from my ear.

A chill ran down my spine as I felt his hand wander down to my bottom. He grabbed as much as would fit in his palm before his other hand grasped onto my neck.

"My kindness only lasts so long. I believe I asked you a question, and when I ask questions, I expect answers—*real* answers," he demanded before harshly letting me go.

I delivered him my best glare and tried to get up from his lap, but he wouldn't allow it.

"Janice," I answered reluctantly.

He was lost in his thoughts before he finally allowed me to get up.

"The stripper?" he asked. I nodded my head in reply. "No. You'll stay here in this room."

"No. No, I can't. At least not for free," I muttered.

A small part of me wasn't an idiot. I knew it was better to be at the huge mansion than in a shelter or out on the streets. I just hoped the decision wasn't something that would come back to bite me later.

"Fine. Five hundred a month will be reduced from the money you earn at my club. Sound 'not for free' enough for you?" he asked, his eyebrow raising in question.

A small smile made its way onto my face as I nodded. "Thank you. I can't belie—"

"Don't thank me quite yet." He smirked.

Then, he grabbed his gun and placed it back into his pants before walking out of the room.

The moment he was gone, sadness hit me like a wrecking ball. His company always managed to make me forget what it was like to be lonely. What was most weird was the fact that I barely knew him at all.

Maybe I was just messed up.

VALENTINO

*W*hat the hell was wrong with me?

Anastasia was all I could think about. From the day I saw her glowing blonde hair on the pole and her plump fuckable lips, I couldn't get rid of the thought of her. She had a way of burning herself into my mind and being too damn stubborn to get out. Even when one of my men handed me a note, written by Dmitri, explaining how he was coming for his daughter, she still heavily occupied my mind. I should have worried more about how close Vincenzo had been getting with the girl, but I couldn't. The whole plan was going to shit, but all I could think about was one blonde girl in particular.

As soon as Valerio notified me of Anastasia at the club on her day off, I knew things weren't good. I didn't completely know her, but I knew her well enough to understand she was not the kind of person to party.

There was a sadness that lurked in her eyes, and I knew it all too well. Never in my life would I openly invite a girl to live in my home. It was rare that I would even bring someone home at all.

It was impossible for me to care for anyone, and I knew that. After failing to care and protect my mother, the last thing I ever wanted to do was fail someone else.

I could only chuckle as I thought about Mama and what she would say about Anastasia. My mother was known for caring for those who couldn't take care of themselves. She had this kindness in her heart that was too pure for the world. Anastasia would make her smile in admiration because she just had this attractive spirit.

Letting out a sigh, I looked at one of my soldiers, Killian. He came to report to me about what had been going on between Vincenzo and Orabella. They were seen going out and together almost every spare moment Vincenzo had. I wanted him to watch her, but I never thought he would grow to like her.

He was too much like Mama. His every decision was focused on his heart, and as much as I wanted to hate that about him. I was envious.

"Watch over Vincenzo and Orabella. I'll handle Dmitri, but for now, put our own threat into motion. Deliver the message that if I even *sense* that he's coming for his daughter, I will kill her," I told one of my soldiers, Killian. He gave me a curt nod before heading for the door.

"Wait!" I called out. He stopped for a quick moment to look at me. "I want you to find out more information about Anastasia Smith. I want to know who her mother is, who her father is, and what happened to her sister."

"Yes, sir. Is that all?" Killian questioned.

"Yes, you are excused," I grumbled.

ANASTASIA

I found myself trying hard to be with Mr. Romano as much as I could. It was getting pretty obvious how much I liked him, even though it wasn't the most logical thing in the world to feel that way.

In the past couple of weeks, he always seemed to be gone. He even stopped talking to me as much. I had to teach my heart that I didn't need the presence of anyone to be happy. Even if that presence was a six-foot-three, black-haired, sexy Italian with delicious abs who knew how to keep me on my toes.

One time, I recalled seeing him walk down the hall with a woman beside him. She had blonde hair and was very tall. Her legs seemed to last forever, and it made me gaze down at my own short legs. The woman was very slim, while my body had some weight in areas. She had a smile to die for, but I could only offer a frown. The woman was gorgeous, but I was far from it.

After that day, I realized that nothing would ever happen between me and Valentino. I learned to avoid him as much as I could. It was easy because he seemed to avoid me too.

Once I let him out of my thoughts, I began to spend most of my time at the strip club, trying to make as much money as possible to be able to move out. My homelessness was probably enough to turn Valentino's interest away. It was the only explanation that made sense.

"Hey, Janice," I said softly as I walked up to her. She was sitting at her station, applying the finishing touches to her white eyeliner.

She looked at me through the mirror and let out a sigh. My shoulders fell in guilt as I watched her lightly set the eyeliner down onto her table.

"I never actually apologized for the way I acted that night. I was just hurt, and what I did felt like the only way to solve everything...I was wrong," I apologized.

She spun around in her chair to face me. A small smile danced on her lips. "I know, and I was only going to give you the petty silent treatment until you actually grew the balls to come to talk to me." She chuckled. "Listen, I never lost someone as close to me as you were to your little sister. If I did, I'm sure I would've acted out in more ways than you did. I'm only looking out for what's best for you because I see you, and I see someone who's lost, but once they're found, the world better prepare for the amount of shit they can do."

I smiled at her words before pulling her in for a hug. She immediately responded by laughing as she wrapped her arms around me.

Once I pulled away, I walked over to the job schedule to see that I was going to be on the floor today while Janice would take the stage. I hated being on the floor, where I had to keep the people who weren't watching the show entertained. Sometimes, that meant lap dances, other times, that meant private dances.

"Looks like you're the star of the night." I winked at her.

"Yeah, yeah." She playfully rolled her eyes.

Together, we exited the back room, ready to do what we had to do. When we got to the entrance of the stage, we bid our goodbyes before separating. I walked out to the floor with a loud sigh. The bright LED lights were blinding and everyone's loud conversations became more prominent.

As soon as the music started and Janice stepped out, men were on their feet, throwing their money at her without giving her the chance to do anything. She wasn't lying when she said that the men loved her.

I headed over to the back, where the secluded people sat in groups. The moment I got there, my heart dropped down to my feet. My sister's doctor was there, laughing with his friends, a drink perched in his hand. I didn't know if I should run or hide, but the options quickly flew out the window when his friend pointed toward me with a smirk.

When the doctor's eyes met mine, his eyes widened as he took in my appearance.

I hurriedly turned around and began to walk away, but he was too quick. His hand hurriedly latched onto my wrist gently.

"Anastasia?"

"*Shit*," I whispered very quietly to myself.

Slowly, I turned around, allowing my embarrassment to be clear on my expression. Recognition immediately made its way onto his face as he looked down my entire body. I understood the temptation in his eyes. My extra small top did a great job of squeezing my breasts to the point that it allowed underboob to make an appearance under the bra. My bottoms were a simple leather thong and the pink boots that were my trademark look only added to the erotic appeal.

"Dr. Flores," I returned.

My gaze wandered over to the group of friends he was with. They seemed to all have been smirking at us.

"Uh, yeah," he muttered, looking over at his friends before

rubbing the back of his neck awkwardly. "I'm here for a bachelor party. I didn't know you worked here. How are you?"

"I'm sorry, but I have to go, okay?" I muttered softly before attempting to turn away from him again, but he wouldn't let go of my wrist. "What do you want from me, a dance or something? I said I gotta go!"

Harshly, I snatched my wrist from his hold. I could tell that he was taken aback by my words, but he nodded his head in understanding. I did feel bad, but the last thing I wanted was anyone judging me. Especially someone who knew Alexandria, and who knew she would never support what I was doing.

I quickly walked off, trying to hold back my tears. In a battle of crying my heart out or continue working as if nothing was happening, my tears were on the verge of winning.

Abruptly, I bumped into a very familiar Italian. His scent hugged me, whispering in my ear that everything would be okay. "Who was that, Bambolina?"

"Who?" I asked, playing dumb before speedily walking right past him. I knew he was following me, but I no longer cared. My body wanted him near me at all times, but my logic was fully aware that he had been avoiding me. It hurt knowing that he wasn't there when I needed him most.

"You know who," he seethed.

I turned around to face him, glaring with narrowed eyes. "A client. Just like there are clients everywhere in this club. I'm not sure if you've forgotten, but I *do* work at a strip club."

He was looking at me with doubt clear in his expression, but I couldn't bring myself to care about his toxicity. I had just seen him with a woman, followed by another one. He had no right to judge me.

"You know better than to—"

"To what? What are you going to do, Mr. Romano? I am one hundred percent sure that nothing you could ever say or do would make me feel any worse than what I feel right now!" I retorted, choking back a sob.

Storming past him, I walked right into the girls' restroom, a place where I knew I was free from everyone.

The moment I saw my eyes in the mirror, I almost broke down. I couldn't shake the feeling as if I were suffocating. It was like my lungs were screaming for air, but no matter how hard I tried to fight—water surrounded me.

A sob ripped out of my throat, followed by another until I found myself just breaking down. I couldn't stand feeling this unfathomable pain, but it was the only way my heart seemed to know how to survive. My heart hurt, and there was no escaping that. No alcohol, no boy, no person could ever heal me in the way Alex could.

"I should be ashamed of myself," I whispered pathetically.

Careful not to ruin my makeup, I used the pad of my fingertips to wipe away the mascara running down my cheeks. I had to take many calming breaths to rid myself of the need to cry again.

Suddenly, my phone began to ring out of nowhere, leaving me to jump in fright. I quickly unzipped my boot and pulled my cell phone out. Just before pressing accept, I made sure that I had sobered up all my tears before putting my phone against my ear.

"Nana," my mum cried into the phone.

Running a hand through my hair, I already knew what was going to happen. She was preparing to tell me that she needed money because of some made-up excuse.

"What?" I huffed out.

A sniffle escaped me before I had a chance to stop it, but of course, she didn't even notice. Even if she did notice it, she didn't bother mentioning it because she didn't want the conversation straying away from her.

"I need help," she sobbed.

My brows pulled together at the desperation in her voice. She'd never sounded so panicked before and it left me worried.

"What? Where are you?" I asked.

I quickly walked out of the restroom before making my way toward the back, where I grabbed my keys and slid on a pair of sweatpants as she told me where to find her. I then exited the club and hurriedly made my way to my car, making her promise to stay on the phone. It was bad for me to leave in the middle of my shift, but I knew I couldn't leave my mother all alone.

I didn't waste any time—just drove off to find her. She informed me that she was outside a small local pet store that she used to take me and Alex to all of the time. The owner once let us play with the pets while our mother went to do whatever it was that she did. I always had the best memories of that place.

My mum was still crying heavily into the phone while I drove, so I pushed on the gas a little harder.

* * *

A LONG DRIVE LATER, I pulled up to the shop and quickly got out. Since my mum didn't give me any specifics about her location other than she was outside our favorite pet shop, it made it hard to find her. It wasn't until I saw a woman lying down in a dark alley, strung out, that I knew it was her.

"What the hell happened?" I asked in shock as I kneeled beside her quivering body. Mum turned to face me, but she looked so drained.

"Nana, I missed you so much. I'm so sorry! I'm so sorry!

Please, don't hate me. You are all I have left," she sobbed. Pulling her against me, I didn't know what to say or do. I just cradled her in my arms, attempting to warm her from the freezing weather.

"Can you stand up?" I asked. She nodded her head before grasping my hand. I got her up and assisted her to my car. When she was slumped against the passenger seat with her seatbelt spread across her body, I got into the driver's side.

"I need help. I'm ready to get help. I'll do anything to be a better mother for you, okay? I'm fucked up, Anastasia. I thought I could get better when I brought you and Alex here away from your dad, but he is always here!" she exclaimed. I started up my car and spared her a sad glance before driving off toward her apartment.

"You never told me what he did to you," I said softly. There was a tug on my heart when the entire atmosphere in the car shifted. My mother didn't respond immediately, almost as if she were taking the time to open permanently sealed doors.

"I went to high school with him. Believe it or not, I was not the type to socialize. My head was always in a book and I learned to be happy with the words I found there," she reminisced. "I met him one night at a party where he got me drunk, and the last thing I remembered was him dragging me up the steps. When I woke up, he was on top of me."

My eyes began to water but I shook it away. I never knew she had to go through so much. It pained me to know that she was living with such trauma and I never had a single clue. *How could I have been so blind?*

"The next day at school, he pretended as if he hadn't done a thing. I tried to tell my mom, but she wouldn't believe me. When I got pregnant, she thought I wasn't worthy of being her daughter. She kicked me out and I had to go from empty house to empty house all on my own," she sniffled. "Years later, I met Alex's dad and he was everything I wanted. He was so kind, and he treated me better than anyone I had ever met. I don't know what happened, but one night, he just left."

Tears dripped down my cheeks, but I continued to drive. Just like life, I had to fight through the tears so I could make it home.

ANASTASIA

"Good morning!" I chirped. "I made you some breakfast."

I was carrying a tray full of food that I had prepared for my mother. It was finally the day everything would change in a positive way for once. My mother had finally accepted that she needed help. That was the first step to recovery, and today would be the next since she would officially be going to rehab.

Her eyes were still shut, and the blanket was slightly pulled down, resting at her waist. Sitting the tray of food down on the nightstand, I began to shake her until her body began to shake wildly of its own accord.

"Mum!" I shouted frightenedly.

She just wouldn't stop and I quickly realized that she was having a seizure. After moving her onto her side, I grabbed my phone and frantically dialed 911. My hands were shaking as I spoke to the operator. The lady was speaking but it sounded like gibberish as I I was trying my best not to panic because I knew she needed me to be strong. As we waited for an ambulance to arrive, my mother's seizure finally stopped.

She still remained unresponsive, and her heartbeat was faint. I held her against my chest, rocking her back and forth, hoping she wouldn't die on me.

Moments later, the ambulance arrived. They must've only taken minutes, but to me, it felt like hours. Every minute that they took, my mother's heartbeat grew weaker. They quickly placed my mum's almost lifeless body onto a stretcher before rolling her into the truck. I tried hard to bite back my tears; I prayed to whoever would listen that my mother was okay.

I couldn't lose her too. I would be without anyone in the world, and I just couldn't let that be. I'd rather have a mother who behaved like a child than a world full of darkness and no one to hold my hand through it all.

I followed closely behind the ambulance all the way to the same hospital where I shared my last moments with my sister.

"Hi, I'm here for Olivia Smith," I immediately said, walking up to the receptionist's desk.

She made me write down my name before telling me to wait in the seating area. Smiling at her, I turned and sat down in a chair. I was tapping my foot against the tile flooring as I patiently waited.

When I came to the realization that it was the same chair I had sat in while they gave me the news of Alex's passing, I shook my head and moved to the seat across.

Moments later, Dr. Flores walked in with a nurse, who was writing things down. His eyes met mine and then he went to tell her something before she nodded her head and walked off. I was praying to whoever would listen that he would just walk away.

Of course, with my terrible luck, he sat down in the chair right beside me instead. My cheeks were a tint of pink as I nervously glanced over at him.

"Anastasia, what brings you here?" he asked.

I turned to look at him and exhaled a long breath that I didn't know I was holding. The whole situation was awkward. He was acting as if he hadn't just practically seen me naked at the strip club.

"My mum had a seizure," I answered honestly.

He nodded his head slowly before a sad look made its way onto his face. I was sure that in his head, he was thinking about how fucked up my life must've been.

"Don't judge me, okay? I don't need your pity for my stripping, my sister, or my mother. I'm fine," I said, running my hand through my hair and crossing one leg over the other.

He didn't say anything, which took me by surprise. When I glanced over at him, he was just looking up at the television broadcasting the news channel.

"That's where you're wrong. I only pity you for the fact that you pity yourself. I'd have to say you are the strongest woman I've ever met, yet you're here with your head held down as if the strongest warriors don't face the biggest challenges," he said.

I couldn't say anything as I just stared at him. He seemed like such a great man, but I had been so cruel to him at the club.

"Let me go check on your mother, and I'll let you know what her doctor says. What's her name?"

A wave of relief flowed through me. Finally, he turned to face me, leaving me to blush for having been caught staring at him. I quickly turned away and faced the television with a blush coating my cheeks.

"Olivia. Olivia Smith," I answered.

He nodded his head with a breathtaking smile on his face. "All right, I'll be right back."

I studied him as he pushed past the doors to the medical

section. Every woman's eyes seemed to follow him when he left. He was the pretty kind of guy but just didn't know it.

* * *

"ANASTASIA," Dr. Flores called out as he gently began to shake me awake. "Wake up."

I could feel my eyelids pulling apart, only for Dr. Flores to enter my sight. His facial expression was what struck my heart in the same way it did when I heard about Alex. I shot up from my seat and gazed at him behind wide eyes, praying that he wasn't going to deliver any more bad news. The last time I fell asleep and was abruptly awoken was the day I lost Alex.

He sighed. "Did you know she uses drugs?"

"Why?" I questioned, suddenly growing defensive.

He let out a huff of air before continuing. "She overdosed. Her doctor, Dr. Reynolds, predicted it was sometime between seven and nine this morning. There was a high dosage of cocaine in her system."

My mother succeeded once again, manipulating me into lowering my defenses for her. She always came through in the end, proving why I shouldn't trust her. I bet she just needed a ride home, and she used me as a pawn with all her lies and sob stories.

"Is she alive? Is she okay?" I pleaded, hating myself for how much I even cared.

"I'm not sure, I wasn't allowed to see her. He was in a rush, but all he said was that she had high dosage of cocaine in her system," he explained.

I was trying my best not to break down again. Tears were something that became part of my everyday ritual. I was so tired of crying my eyes out.

"This is the challenge, huh? How many more challenges

do I have to go through just to be left alone? Why do I have to be the strong one?" I protested. "She should be the strong one! *She* is my mother!"

I didn't bother to wait for a reaction. Everyone in that hospital probably thought I was insane, and maybe I was. So, I got up and walked out of the hospital, ready to just disappear like my mother had done many times.

When I arrived at my car, I was grabbed by the wrist. Tension enveloped my body, but it was quick to ease when I saw it was Dr. Flores. "Don't do anything stupid, okay? Look, none of this is fair, and I know that. Think about Alexandria, and what she would want you to do. I truly mean it when I say I see a lot of strength in you, Anastasia."

I didn't know what to say or do. I knew he was right about everything, but I just couldn't bring myself to acknowledge that. I knew Alex would want me to stay and feed into my mother's lies, but I couldn't. I was suffocating, and I wanted to go somewhere that would allow me to breathe.

So, just like that, I turned around and got into my car. I didn't bother to spare him a single glance as I took off.

I continued to drive until I made it to the mansion, where I practically ran into the house, ignoring Sarah, who looked worried at my appearance. There was no one I wanted to hear from. She seemed to pick up on the fact that I didn't want to talk because she didn't say a word as I made my way to my room.

There was nothing in the world that I hated more than the thought of being alone. It was my biggest fear, one that lodged itself into my every thought. I was weak. Dr. Flores could lie and say there was strength in me, but he was wrong. He wasn't aware of the many times I cried myself to sleep. That man had no clue how many memories would surface in my brain of the loving family I once had before everything fell apart. Dr. Flores didn't know me well enough to assume there was even the slightest bit of strength in me when my strength relied on the people I loved. Those same people either died, or they were *destroying* me.

A sob burst out of me as my shoulders moved to accommodate every sharp inhale. It confused me to say that I hated my mum to the point that I couldn't hate her at all. I wanted her to be okay just as much as I craved for her to suffer just like she had been forcing me to do for many years.

"Anastasia?" Mr. Romano's voice asked as he carefully entered my room. I didn't even realize he was home, but there he was, Valentino Romano. I gazed up into his beautiful blue eyes, forgetting about the tears still rolling down my cheek.

He grabbed onto my hands and pulled me into his chest. When he pressed his soft lips to the top of my head, I could just feel myself shutting my eyes. I didn't say anything, he just held me. I found myself crying in his arms as he ran his hand through my hair.

"What tore my Bambolina apart?" he asked, sounding deeply concerned. His words only seemed to make me cry harder. I didn't know if he actually cared, or if he was just asking to be considerate. All I knew was that with his arms around me, I'd never felt more secure.

Valentino patiently waited for me to stop crying. I was grateful for his patience. He just continued to stroke my hair while his other hand moved up and down my back. Valentino was comforting me in a way that I never wanted to let go.

"I lost my baby sister to cancer not too long ago," I tested, pausing to see if Valentino would stop me, or tell me that he didn't care about my life. When he didn't say a word, I continued. "I thought that it would change my mum for the better, but it didn't. She's still the same woman who ruined my life, and now she's in the hospital, and I can't stop caring even though I know she never even *bothered* to think about Alex."

Moments passed. Valentino never stopped his hand that moved against my back, and I was grateful for that.

"I know what it feels like to lose a mother and a sister," he said softly. My brows pulled together as I gazed at him. There was an extra thump to my heart at the sound of him finally opening up to me.

"What happened?" I asked, *needing* to know more about him

He let out a loud sigh, his eyes going blank as if he were thinking about a distant memory. Just when I thought he was going to share a piece of his heart that he kept locked away, he shook his head and gazed out in the distance. "Doesn't matter. I was young when I realized that happiness only belonged in fairytales."

"I guess so," I whispered, disappointed, allowing my hand to fall from his grasp. *He was never going to open up to me. .*

He cleared his throat. "I will be gone for a few weeks. I wanted to stop by and let you know. See you soon, Bambolina."

"See you soon." I smiled even though my heart called for him to stay.

ANASTASIA

*S*tepping out of the shower, I let a small smile melt onto my face. Two weeks blew away from me, but I was glad for the time I spent to try and evolve emotionally. Not a day went by without me thinking of Alexandria, but I did my best to begin the process of healing.

Even her doctor, Jacob Flores, managed to help me in a way. We had gotten closer, and I was grateful to have him as a friend. He would listen to me talk for hours, and he always offered the best advice. Jacob was such an amazing man, and I was glad he was in my life.

Not only that, but my mother was finally getting better. She was in rehab and had been writing to me every day. The mother I grew up with was returning to me, and I only wished Alex could see it.

I finished curling the last few strands of my hair before I collided with something hard.

"Bambolina," Valentino said.

My widened eyes went up to meet him in shock. I don't think I expected him to return so soon.

I was only wearing a towel, and his presence made me

cling onto it tighter. It would take only one tug for me to be completely bare, and I wasn't sure if I wanted that.

Out of nowhere, his lips came down to meet mine. Butterflies fluttered around in my stomach, begging me to pull him closer, but I couldn't. I didn't even get to say two words before he was prancing on me like some booty call. I tried to break away, but that didn't stop his lips from wandering down my neck.

My gaze strayed in front of me as a loud sigh fell from my lips. Everything was always so sexual with him, and I was tired of it. Pushing him away, I strolled out of the restroom, entering my room, where I turned around and put on a pair of panties without taking off the towel. The sound of Valentino's footsteps didn't go unnoticed, but I simply ignored him.

"I just got back, and this is how you treat me?" he teased.

I continued to ignore him as I took off my towel with my back facing him. I quickly put on a white crop top before sliding on a pair of blue jean shorts.

He walked up to me and grabbed my hips from behind before pulling me against his own. I couldn't stop myself from rolling my eyes when his lips connected with my neck.

"Why are you getting dressed?" he questioned. He reached to my front, where he started to undo my shorts. His lips moved up from my neck to my jawline.

"Mr. Romano—"

"Valentino," he corrected, annoyed.

I knew he wanted me to call him by his name, but calling him by his professional name was the only thing that made sense. It helped remind me that it was all our relationship would ever be—*professional*. It shouldn't be anymore than that.

"I have to go," I muttered.

"Where? Another date with that doctor?" he asked.

I turned around to face him with narrowed eyes. There was absolutely no emotion on his face and it killed me. I could never comprehend how he could seem so emotionless.

"Are you stalking me now?" I questioned.

He didn't say anything, leaving me to scoff and push right past him. No more words were exchanged as I opened my door and headed out. I made sure to slam the door shut behind me as I strolled down the hallway.

It had been two weeks since I last heard from him, and I couldn't understand why he thought it was okay to greet me in such a sexual way. I wasn't some prostitute who served him for living in his home. I especially didn't want to be viewed as such by him.

I made it to the kitchen, where Sarah was talking to a raven-haired girl. From the back of her, she kind of looked like Alex. It caused me to fall into a deep state of confusion. I just stared at her, hoping I wasn't seeing something that wasn't there.

"Anastasia," Sarah greeted behind a small smile.

"Hey!" I chirped. Then, I turned to look at the girl Sarah had been talking to. "What do we have here, a new recruit?"

"No, this is Orabella. Orabella, meet Anastasia," Sarah had introduced.

"Nice to meet you, Orabella. You know, if you ever get bored around here, I'd be more than happy to teach you a new way of life. Maybe a little stripping, or just casually hanging out. I get bored around here sometimes," I told her with a grin.

Her face brightened with joy.

"You know, actually, I was just about to head out to see a friend. Do you want to join me?" I asked her. Sarah grimaced at my words, leaving my brows to pull together. *What was her problem?*

"Yes, please," Orabella said desperately. With a huge smile

spreading across my face, I grasped her hand into my own and led her to the front door.

She kept glancing behind her as we walked, but instead of speaking up about it, she followed me outside and we headed to my car. When I glanced at Orabella, I noticed her gaze was off somewhere else. She looked like a scared puppy who was about to pee on themselves.

Looking off in the direction she'd been staring at, I noticed Valentino was angrily heading directly to us...to *me*.

"Why would you bring her out here? Do you know what you've just done?" Valentino spat, his teeth clenching with anger.

"I don't understand," I whispered, my brows furrowing.

"This is Vincenzo's girl. She is not allowed out of that house unless he's with her," he explained.

My eyes widened. Vincenzo was the boss, the *don*. He made ruthless decisions every day, and the last thing I needed was to be on his bad side. I couldn't comprehend why she couldn't leave the house without Mr. Rossi, but I knew better than to question them. Their business was none of mine.

"I didn't know," I gasped.

"I'll take care of my brother, but you—you owe me." He smirked before letting me go and dragging Orabella back into the house. He was nowhere near gentle as he manhandled her. I felt bad for the poor girl. For some reason, I felt like there was more to the story.

THE DRIVE to Jacob's house was short, seeing as he owned a huge place not very far from where I stayed. Once I was parked outside, Jacob walked out with a huge smile on his face. I stepped out of my car and quickly strolled over to embrace him in a hug.

"Hey, Jake!" I laughed.

"I thought we talked about you no longer calling me that." He rolled his eyes as he pulled away from me. I laughed, wandering over to his front door, where I opened it as if I owned the place. Being an oncologist must've meant big money—his house was huge. The best part of it all was that he owned and lived in it all by himself.

"You're not innocent. My sister insisted that you call her Alex, yet you always called her Alexandria," I pointed out.

He nodded his head slowly as a tint of pink made its way onto his cheeks. "I am terrible with names. Once I call someone something, it just sticks and there's no changing it with me."

I laughed before sitting down on top of his couch. He wasn't slow to join as he plopped down beside me.

"Max!" I yelled out right after I began making kissing noises with my lips.

As expected, the loud sound of nails clacking against the tile echoed through the room as the huge boxer jumped on top of me. He quickly began to lick the side of my face as I cringed away. His tail was wagging happily as he continued his assault.

"Hi, Max," I gushed. His tail began to wag faster while I laughed at him. He was my favorite part of going over to Jacob's place.

"Are you still available to watch him this weekend while I go to a meeting in Vegas? The house will be all yours," he promised.

I pretended to think about it for a second before a huge grin broke out onto my face. "Of course, I'll watch Max! Just go do your thing, Doc."

My fingers skimmed through Max's soft fur as his wet nose touched my cheek.

"Have you been talking to your mom?" he asked.

I nodded. "Yes, every day. I told her about you and she said she'd like to meet you," I answered.

His brow rose as a small smile tugged on his lips. "I can't believe you actually spoke about me. I thought you hated me."

"I don't hate you, Jacob." I laughed. "If I hated you, I wouldn't be in your house."

"Touché to that." He chuckled.

My phone had been ringing constantly in my pocket. At first, I ignored it and continued to pet Max, but after a while I couldn't anymore; it seemed too emergent. Knotting my eyebrows together, I pulled out my phone to see that I had several messages from Janice. Each message notified me how pissed Valentino was.

"Hey, um, I have to go," I muttered before sliding my phone back into my pocket.

A huge smile broke out on his face again as he opened his arms out wide. I hurriedly walked up to him to embrace him in our second hug. He always managed to give the best hugs.

As I was pulling away, I muttered, "Bye, Jakey, and thank you for helping me return to a stable mentality."

"What are friends for?" he questioned with a grin. I smiled before turning and walking toward the dog, where I ruffled his fur playfully.

"Bye, Maxy!" I exclaimed, bending down and kissing his snout.

Just as soon as I exchanged my goodbyes, I got back into my vehicle and raced home.

* * *

WHEN I ENTERED THE MANSION, I searched everywhere for any sign of life. Not even Sarah was in the kitchen, which was odd.

Maybe if I moved fast enough to creep back into my room, no one would see me. I could avoid Valentino's wrath as well as the don's.

Speed-walking all the way to my room, I entered and quickly shut the door behind me. When I turned around, Valentino was already on my bed, anger shedding off of him in waves.

"Oh, shit!" I gasped, clutching my hand against my chest. He startled me, and the fast pace of my heart was proof.

"So, tell me, Bambolina, where were you?" he asked.

I ignored him and tried to casually head to the bathroom so I could lock the door until he decided to leave, but he was quick to grab me and throw me on top of the bed. Alcohol was present on his breath.

"I was with a friend," I told him. He scoffed before walking over to me. I had to prop myself onto my elbows to be able to look at him.

"The fucking doctor? Do you think I'm stupid?" he questioned.

Just as I was about to open my mouth to speak, his hands grabbed onto my thighs and pulled them apart. He was on top of me in a second. I was exhilarated, but I didn't allow myself to forget that I needed to stand up for myself.

"So what? Just because I'm a woman and you're a man, that entitles you to have friends, but I can't?" I quizzed.

His eyes narrowed. He knew I was right, but his pride wouldn't allow him to admit it. Without another word, he got off of me and exited the room. I couldn't seem to grasp what his problem was.

I exhaled a breath that I didn't know I was holding. Valentino was such a confusing man.

Placing my phone on the bed, I strolled over to the restroom. With my hands on the sink, I let out a loud groan. Guilt was starting to seep into my heart, and I hated myself for being so sensitive. He had been drinking, and I had never seen him so distressed.

My mind kept replaying the time I had gotten drunk, and the way he was there for me. He had shown me a lot of kindness, and the least I could do was talk to him.

"Don't do it, Anastasia," I whispered to myself as I felt the need to apologize.

Throwing open the bathroom door, I exited my room and made my way down the hall. My first stop was his office, but when I pushed the door open—he wasn't there. So, I decided to go up two sets of stairs toward his bedroom. While he was away, I found myself wandering the mansion out of boredom. One day, I stumbled upon a room, and based on the scent, I knew it belonged to Valentino.

Once I opened his door, I walked in, and heard the sound of running water. He must've been in the shower, so like he always did to me—I sat down on his bed to wait.

His bed was much comfier than mine. It was also a lot bigger. Not only that, but his room was two times the size of my room, and it didn't shed even an ounce of light.

My eyebrows came together as I looked on the floor, where a full folder of all kinds of papers and images sat. Just as I was about to reach down to read it, the shower turned off. I quickly sat down on the bed and pulled out my phone, as if I hadn't been attempting to snoop.

Seconds later, the door opened. He had a towel wrapped around his lower region and a toothbrush in his hand. At first he didn't seem to notice me and was about to remove his towel before a loud squeal shot out of me. His eyes met mine while his hand paused on top of his towel.

Then, he did an absolutely unexpected thing by removing

the towel, leaving me to quickly cover my eyes with my hand.

"What do you want?" he asked.

I moved my fingers apart on my face to catch a glance of him, still very naked.

"I wanted to apologize," I muttered, my cheeks coated a bright pink when he turned around and caught me staring. He walked over to me, leaving my heartbeat to increase. I tried to look at anything other than his huge dick, but I failed.

"You keep staring. You want to go for a ride?" he asked. I let out a loud sigh, standing up as I did. "No, stay. I know how badly you want to."

"I don't understand where your huge ego came from, but no, I don't want you," I seethed, not knowing if I was lying or telling the truth.

"You say you don't want me, Bambolina. How many times are you going to tell yourself that until you actually start to believe it? If you didn't want me, you wouldn't be right here. You wouldn't be..." His hand entered my shorts, where he made it to my dripping lips. "...wet."

My finger crept up his abs and to his chest, where I caressed his skin. A smirk made its way onto my face at the realization that I had a plan to turn the whole conversation back on him. "Let's not forget that you want me. How long have I had this dramatic effect on you? You can try to hide it all you want, but I know you do have feelings."

He grabbed me by my neck and kissed me harshly. His hands went down to my shorts. He pushed away the fabric until it was on the floor. I tried to respond to his kissing, but he was attempting to get his message across, the kiss was too dominant to be returned.

He grabbed my thighs as he lifted me up so I was straddling his waist. His hand moved over to the back of my neck, pulling my head away from his.

"Do I want to fuck you? Yes. That's all," he growled, inches away from my swollen lips. I got down and picked up my shorts before rolling my eyes.

"Keep telling yourself that," I told him before walking over to his door and leaving without another word.

ANASTASIA

"*H*ey, Mom," I said.

She walked up to me and embraced me in a hug. I smiled as I wrapped my arms around her in return.

"Hey, I wasn't expecting you," she said as she began to pull away.

Her therapist cleared her for a walk with me around the garden at the rehabilitation facility, it felt good to finally be able to visit her. A sense of pride ran through my body as I looked at her. She was healthier, with weight filling out her body. I couldn't be prouder.

"Yeah, I decided to drop by and do a surprise visit before work." I smiled.

It wasn't exactly a lie. The truth was I needed some motherly advice on how to go about the whole Valentino situation. After last night, everything I felt for him intensified. It had gotten to the point where I couldn't even sleep properly. *Was he right about me having feelings for him?*

"Something is bothering you. What's wrong?" she asked.

I grabbed her hand and sat her down on a bench that overlooked all of the beautiful flowers. It smelled like my favorite scent in the entire world—a mix of nature and warmth.

"It's about a guy," I began. Her eyebrows rose, and I watched as she prepared herself to open her mouth. "No, it's not Jacob. It's another guy, his name is Valentino."

"What happened to Jacob? I thought you guys were hitting it off," she said. I gave her a pointed look before turning to face the garden, letting out an exhale.

"No, Mom, Jacob and I are just friends," I explained.

She let out a chuckle before nodding her head. My hand reached out for her delicate one, and I smiled as I caressed her skin.

"Valentino, on the other hand, is a bit more complex. We've done things that are too weird to talk to you about, but that's all it ever is, you know? It's hard to explain, but I'm so tired of acting like I don't want to be with him in a way that is more than lust when it's beginning to be all I think about," I explained, sounding as complicated as I felt. "He's so infuriating. I know he feels the same way, yet he hasn't made a single move. He's cocky and condescending, and everything I hate in a guy, but I don't understand why I can't stop thinking about him."

When I gazed into the eyes of my mother, I saw the understanding hidden in them. She was wearing a smile on her face before her hand clasped mine. "Do you love him, Nana?"

"What? No!" I quickly exclaimed. She gave me a pointed look before deciding to just shrug it off. Of course, I didn't *love* him, I absolutely hated him sometimes. I hated the way he made me feel emotionally and the way he knew just what to say in order to keep me on my toes. I hated how good he made my body feel. I hated how much I knew deep down that I didn't really hate him at all.

Her hand never let go of mine and a feeling surged through me at the realization that I never wanted her to.

I rested my head on her shoulder and wished everything could pause for a moment. The breeze that floated through my hair, and the rich smell of peace calmed me. Even my heart seemed to beat in a harmonious way. I hadn't felt this amount of freedom and relaxation in months.

"There's not a day that goes by where I don't think about Alex," my mother said. "I wasn't there to watch her last breath. I cared more about drugs than my dying little girl."

She began to sob.

I pressed my lips against her cheek. We sat there drowning in our own thoughts while the brisk wind blew past us. She whispered, "I love you, Anastasia. I promise to be as strong as you have been for this entire family."

VALENTINO

I heard the door to the estate close, alerting me that my brother and the girl, Orabella, had left the house. I should have known that Vincenzo was losing his heart to the girl. My brother was the type to do that sort of thing—dating, marriage, having kids. I, on the other hand, preferred the better side of things—making money, fucking, having women.

My brother's happiness meant a lot to me, but Dmitri deserved to pay for what he had done. I hoped Enzo's heart wouldn't get in the way of my plan. He could fuck her as he saw fit, but the time to set the plan into motion was coming soon. Very soon.

It didn't take me long to enter the club. The first thing that caught my eyes was Anastasia. She was on the pole wearing her pink plastic-like lingerie set with heels to match.

From the moment I met her, I knew she would do a phenomenal job. It was the way men seem captivated by her appeal—it's what captivated me.

"Mr. Romano," a girl purred out, coming up to me with a tray of shot glasses. She had nothing on except nipple coverings and a thong. I reached over and grabbed a glass of whatever drink she was serving.

Just as she was about to walk off, I grabbed her by her wrist.

"Tell Barbie she has a private dance, VIP room," I whispered in her ear before delivering a wink. She looked over at the stage where Barbie was finishing up her dance with hateful eyes before nodding her head.

"Anything for you, sir," she said seductively.

I downed the whole drink as the girl walked off. My gaze settled on Anastasia. Without even looking, I could tell the men in the audience couldn't take their eyes of her. Little did they know, she was mine. *All mine.*

* * *

IT DIDN'T TAKE LONG for Anastasia to make an appearance. The entire room was dark except for the pink lights that lit up the stripper pole.

I watched her walk in with her blonde hair cascading down her back in waves as she walked up to the pole. Slow music began to play in the background as her hand slowly graced the metal pole.

"You asked for a taste of Barbie?" she asked, her sexy accent falling off of her tongue as her big breasts spilled out of her tight bra.

My tongue swept over my lips at the thought of bending her over and doing more than tasting her. My dick began to harden. I watched as she spun around the pole, clasping it as she dragged herself up. Her legs pulled apart in the splits. Her body spun, giving me a view of her entire body.

My favorite part was when she spread her long legs in the shape of a *V*, showing me everything she had to offer. It was such an erotic sight, and it'd be a lie to say it didn't make me want more of her.

After that, she climbed down the pole leisurely, crawling off the small stage toward me. It took everything inside of me to not reach out and grab her boobs, as they were begging me to relieve their restraints.

When she was in front of me, I watched as she turned her body, placing herself onto my lap.

She smelled like vanilla, and it hit me strongly as she moved her hair to the side. She gyrated her hips against me, creating that friction I'd always wanted from her.

Then, she bent over and began to bounce her sweet ass to the beat of the music, expertly aiming for my hardening shaft. She grinded her hips against mine, going slow at first before speeding up.

I watched as her hands moved behind her back. At first, I wasn't sure what she was doing, but when the sound of her bra being undone hit my ears it made me a smirk.

"Careful there, Bambolina." I chuckled darkly. Her body tensed up on top of me, causing my smirk to grow.

"I had a feeling it was *you*," she spat distastefully.

"Don't sound so disappointed." I chuckled. She rolled her eyes before she began to get up, but my hands closed on her waist, keeping her in place.

"Don't leave now, it was just beginning to get fun," I whispered in her ear.

She placed her hand on my chest as I brought her in closer. My hand came up and tugged at her undone bra, which she quickly grasped, rushing to hold it against her chest.

"What do you want, Mr. Romano?" she asked.

"Valentino," I corrected, annoyed, before grabbing her hands away from her bra. She tried to pull away from my grip, but I wasn't having it.

"I have to go," she said, trying to get up once again.

"See, that's the thing, *Barbie*. I'm supposed to be *'handling'* you right now. My brother was very upset about the whole Orabella thing." I smirked, loving how her fear and nervousness was visibly noticeable in her face as it skyrocketed.

"I promise I won't screw up anymore, Valentino," she pleaded.

My dick twitched at the sound of my name coming from her mouth. Her body was right against mine, her sex mere pieces of fabric away. The temptation was screaming at me, and it all began with her.

"Persuade me," I whispered, my voice getting deeper with lust.

She stared into my eyes for a long moment before she got down on the floor. I watched as she unbuttoned my trousers before unzipping them.

"Only if you want to," I muttered as my eyes found hers.

"I do."

All I wanted from her was to continue her dance, but with her now on her knees in front of me—*who was I to say no?*

Her hand found my length, and she stroked it from the outside of my boxers, making me groan. When she pulled back the waistband of my boxers to pull my entire length out, I couldn't take my eyes off of her.

"I've never done this before, so don't expect me to be an expert or anything," she said softly before gazing up into my eyes. Her words were like music to my ears. I loved the thought of bring her first of anything.

Anastasia's hand began to move against my shaft until I felt the wet, warm, and moist sensation of her mouth on my cock. I closed my eyes at the feel of her full lips sliding down my entire length. She then came back up with my cock head in her lovely mouth. Her soft tongue was circling around my shaft as her long, blonde hair hung down, brushing against my balls.

"*Merda*. Don't stop," I groaned.

She then began sucking me into her mouth even harder and made sure to bob her head up and down furiously. Her tongue moved around me, and it felt like I was in heaven as I grew bigger and bigger in her mouth. The head of my cock was hitting her throat as it squeezed around me.

After she began stroking my balls with her hand, she made a slurping noise as she inhaled my swollen shaft, driving me to the edge very quickly. Grasping her silky strands of hair, I lifted my hips up to sink my cock deeper in her throat before I shot a long stream of cum into her mouth. My Bambolina pulled my cock out and pumped the rest of my cum into her open mouth, sucking me dry.

When she finished, I watched her as she tucked me back into my boxers and got up from the floor. Her eyes were on mine, and I'm sure she could see that it only made me want her more. Grabbing a hold of her arm, I brought her closer, so she was mere inches from my face.

"Did you lie to me when you said you've never done it before?" I asked, growing angry.

"What do I have to lie for?" she questioned. I let go of her arm before standing up directly in front of her. Her eyes were leveled with my chest before she finally craned her neck up to look into my eyes.

I never would've thought an amateur could've given me the best head I'd ever received. It was obvious she wasn't lying because my men searched her thoroughly. She was always so busy, Anastasia never had time for any boy. However, watching those men lust after her and knowing that any guy could ask her for a private dance where she would show them everything that belonged to me was what drove me mad.

"As your punishment for lying and what the *Don* has agreed is very reasonable, your dances are canceled for the week. You're staying in my wing of the mansion until further notice, and you're not to leave it. Do I make myself clear, Bambolina?" I asked.

"But I—"

"It was going to be far worse," I finished for her before walking toward the door. As I left, I zipped and buttoned back up my trousers with a smirk on my face.

A week of fun.

ANASTASIA

*V*alerio forced me to leave the club the moment I walked in. It seemed as though Valentino had told him what he planned. His punishment was delirious. He just wanted an excuse to keep me from making money. I was mostly upset because I had already gotten dressed to work, and it was all for nothing.

Storming over to his room, I slammed open the door and grabbed Valentino by his tie. He didn't look at all surprised to see me because he was wearing his stupid smirk on his face as his hands came down to my hips. Even his eyes flashed down to my exposed breasts as he waited for my outburst.

"You think you're so cool, don't you?" I asked angrily. "I'm not staying in this room. I have responsibilities, and I need to make money! You are such an asshole!"

"You'll still be making money. Think of it as paid time off." He smiled. I rolled my eyes before pushing his hands away.

"Thanks, but no thanks, Mr. Romano," I scoffed sarcastically. With eyes so cold and one arm wrapped around my waist, he grabbed me by my hair sinfully.

"Call me that again," he dared.

I narrowed my eyes at him. My brain told me not to, but my lust was begging me to say it.

"Mr. Romano." I smirked. My smirk didn't last long because he spun me around and pressed me into the wall. I could feel his hard-on present on my bottom. His hand grabbed a hold of my neck, where he pushed my upper half against his chest.

Valentino's teeth came down and bit my earlobe before going lower to my neck, leaving to the frenzy of butterflies in my stomach. The hand that was around my waist had moved up to my bra, pushing past it.

"How about I fuck you so hard you would have no choice but to stop forgetting my name, Anastasia?" he whispered into my ear, leaving a chill to run down my spine.

His hand reached over to where he ripped the thin mesh bra. A gasp climbed out of me when his hand quickly went to massage my breast.

"Tell me, how many men have you slept with?" he asked.

His lips found my neck, and he began to kiss my skin. I knew that the moment he found out I never had sex with anyone, he wouldn't want me in the same way. I was sure that most of the women he slept with were experienced.

"No one," I whispered truthfully, but with shame.

He pulled his head away from my neck before turning me around to face him. I was too scared to know what was going through his head. There was an emptiness in his eyes, leaving nothing for my mind to comprehend.

"Lay down," he ordered.

I didn't bother to disobey him as I laid down on his bed. My eyes never left his as he took off his suit jacket and began to unbutton his shirt before throwing that off as well.

"Valentino," I began. He didn't hear a word coming from my mouth, instead, he latched onto my neck. I could feel his lips depositing kisses everywhere. His warm skin felt so great against mine.

His hands latched onto his slacks, and he pushed them off of his body. Taking a huge gulp of air, I looked down at the only piece of fabric dividing us and it was his underwear. I watched him lean over to grab a condom after he removed his briefs.

He kissed down my body all the way to my pussy, where he pulled my legs apart. His finger gently massaged my walls, leaving me to close my eyes at the intensity.

I moaned while his finger worked my insides. Then, he continued to kiss down to the dip between my legs, where he kissed my clit. When he pulled out his fingers, his tongue entered me. My eyes shut as my back arched against the intrusion. A shudder ran through my body at the feel of his tongue stroking my clit. He was sucking, nibbling, biting, and I was enjoying every sensation.

As he tongued me, he made sure to use his finger to pump in and out of me. My body was convulsing on his tongue and finger, but when it dove so deep between my walls, I lost it. I quickly came on his tongue. He smirked against my clit before kissing back up my body. It wasn't until he was at my jaw that his arm wrapped around my waist, where he pinned me in place.

"You ready for me, baby?" he asked huskily. The head of his shaft was toying with my clit. I could feel my lower region throbbing for him as I nodded my head.

The feel of his hand running down my thigh didn't go unnoticed when he hooked it around his waist. Carefully, he pushed into my body. He made sure to take his time, cherishing me by entering with only a few inches.

Every time he pushed in a little more of himself, I

grimaced in pain. The feel of my body expanding to compensate for his size was what hurt the most. It seemed to go like that for a while until he was completely inside of me.

His eyes stared into my own as he began to pump his full girth into my patient body. It hurt, but the more he worked himself inside of me, the less pain I felt.

Soon, I was moaning in pleasure. He seemed to take my moans as encouragement because he began to move faster and harder into my body. I didn't even know it was possible to move that fast. My walls were massaging his shaft as he entered me, hitting my g-spot every time.

My eyes found his, only to see he was looking at me intensely before his gaze fell down to my lips. I leaned up and kissed him deeply as he continued to thrust madly into me.

"Valentino," I moaned as I broke the kiss.

His lips roamed down to my breast, where he pulled the bud in between his teeth before circling his tongue around my nipple. Biting down onto my lip, I grabbed onto his hair and let out a screech as he found a spot so deep within me that my leg almost shook.

"You feel so tight," he groaned.

Every time he was inside of me, my core would squeeze around him until he pulled out, and then would do the same once he returned. After a while, I felt my body on the edge of coming.

"Oh, I'm close," I told him.

My body quickly convulsed around him until I came right on top of his cock. After a few more strokes, he began to slow down until he pulled out of me and removed his condom.

"That was so good," I stated.

I sat up on the bed and kissed him with everything I had to offer. He responded by wrapping his arms around my waist and pulling me closer. My mouth was openly inviting him to do as he wanted.

"Let's go for a ride," I told him, smirking at my offer.

Reaching over, I grabbed one of his condoms and handed it to him. He used his teeth to take it out of the package before placing it on.

My lips found his neck, where I decided to leave a hickey like he always managed to do to me. My hand roamed over his chest until I made it to his semi-erect penis covered by a condom. Placing my mouth over it, I circled my tongue around the head before the bland taste of a condom entered my mouth.

The moment my mouth engulfed his hardening erection, it shot up. He was hard as a rock and my mouth took full advantage of that. Then, I pulled away to watch his hungry eyes. He wasn't saying a word, he just watched my every movement.

A smirk spread across my face before I turned around and straddled him. Slowly, I lowered myself onto his thick pole until my bottom was connected to his hips. He let out a loud groan as he smacked my butt.

My hips moved against his while his hands squeezed my ass. When I slid up his shaft, I came back down, letting out a moan as I did so. Every time I came down onto his cock, my hips made sure to grind against his balls. His groans only seemed to turn me on more.

"Go faster," he demanded.

I tried to do my best, but it only caused my ass to jiggle with each thrust. After a while of attempting to go faster, he lifted his hips off the bed and began to pummel into my body. My eyes were rolling to the back of my head as he pumped in and out of me at an inhuman speed. His hand reached over and gripped my hair as he arched my back.

He then leaned up, so my back was pressed against his

front. His hands wandered up from my bottom to my boobs, where he fondled them, all while thrusting into my body as if his life counted on it.

"Valentino," I gasped.

His lips found my neck, where he left open-mouthed kisses until once again, I came hard. I felt my whole body let out all its sexual frustration.

He continued to use my body until he finished. Slowly, he picked me up off of his cock and laid me down before throwing away his second condom of the night.

"Round three?" he asked.

I looked over at him behind exhausted eyes before smiling.

VALENTINO

$\mathcal{I}$ had visualized having Anastasia in so many ways, but I never pictured it like this. After I had lost count of how many different positions I had her in, she fell asleep. I gazed at her face as her full lips parted in the sexiest way. Her arm subconsciously wrapped around my waist as her face buried itself into my neck. She let out the calmest sigh against me.

My mind was hazy as I replayed our previous events over and over. I never would've anticipated her to be such a freak. My hand caressed her soft hair that always managed to smell like vanilla. She moved closer to me, and I trailed my hand lower from her hair and over to cup her ass. It might be attached to her, but it was all mine.

My other hand moved over to the other side of me to switch off the light. When I was back in position, my eyes trained themselves on the ceiling.

Grabbing Anastasia, I placed her head on top of my chest before allowing my hand to wander up from her ass to her waist, where I held her against me.

Once again, I found my way through her hair as I thought

about what my mother would think of her. She'd probably say she was beautiful with a personality that kept me in check, and I'd agree.

Everything was always so unexpected when it came to the blonde-haired Australian. She was amusing. The only thing I disliked was her love-sick doctor, who must've not understood me when I told him to back off. It seemed like I would have to pay him another visit.

"Alex," she whispered, her hold on me tightening.

I froze before glancing down at her, knowing exactly who she was calling for...her sister.

As strong as Anastasia seemed, she was delicate. Like a glass, one drop and she'd break, but the pieces of broken glass were ready to pierce skin and leave someone to bleed.

Before I allowed exhaustion to take over, I made a promise to myself. Yes, I let my mother go, and I let my sister go, but Anastasia would forever and always stay.

* * *

AFTER WAKING UP, I quickly realized Anastasia was still sleeping peacefully on top of me. I quietly picked her up and laid her on the other side of the bed before going into the shower. Mist danced around me as I stepped underneath the spray of water. My hand went up to run through my hair. Then, I felt arms wrap around my waist.

Turning around, my eyes met the blue crystal stare of Anastasia. I wrapped my arm around her neck before pulling her into my chest.

"I want you right here," I said.

Her eyes looked up into mine before grabbing my shampoo and placing it in her hands. I watched as she lathered it in her hair.

"I'm sore," she said.

"Aw, did I make my Bambolina sore?" I asked sarcastically before snatching my shampoo from her hands and placing it in my own. She narrowed her eyes at me as she began to rinse her soapy hair.

When she was finished, I grabbed her by the arm and placed her outside of the shower. She let out a huff of annoyance, but I was too busy to be distracted with her. It was already bad enough I spent the whole night in bed with her instead of worrying about Dmitri. I was scared that if she looked at me too long, I would fuck her and never stop.

"You are such an asshole," she groaned.

I listened to her walk away as I continued to shower, but I knew she hadn't left because the door still remained closed. Rolling my eyes, I prepared for her to throw a tantrum.

"I bet Jacob wouldn't mind letting me shower with him," she pointed out. Her words were constantly replaying in my mind, pissing me off repeatedly.

I stepped out of the shower and narrowed my eyes. I noticed that she had already wrapped herself up in a towel.

"What the fuck did you just say to me?" I asked.

She bit down on her lip as her blue eyes pierced into mine with her head held high. "I *said* that I bet Jacob wouldn't mind letting me shower with *him*."

I snatched her towel off before dragging her back into the shower. Slamming her against the shower door, I grabbed her by the neck and pinned her to the wall. All I could see was red as I looked down at her.

"You think you're sore now?" I asked before bringing my face close to her own. She didn't say anything as her eyes continued to focus on mine. 'Wait until you feel this."

Turning her around, I bent her over. My hands were already in her hair as I pulled her toward me, leaving her back to arch.

"Val—"

I reached over and grabbed her throat just as I entered her raw. Her pussy hugged me tightly as I pumped into her.

"Oh," she began to moan, but I cut her off by smacking her juicy ass that belonged to me. Not Jacob, not even the thirsty men at my club, but *me*.

"Shut the fuck up!" I ordered.

She turned her head a bit to look at me from over her shoulder. With a smirk on my face, my hand came down onto her ass once again, only harder. She flinched slightly, but bit down on her lip to keep from saying anything else.

I was rocking in and out of her body way harder than I had ever fucked anyone before. My anger consumed me, and her pussy was my only outlet. I could feel her knees beginning to grow weak, so I lifted her up against the glass and continued fucking her sweet pussy from behind. Again, my hand came down to smack her ass over and over until my hand was stinging.

When I looked down at my work, a grin formed on my face at the sight of the red handprint on her bottom.

Turning her around, I lifted her, so her legs were wrapped around my waist.

I bit down on her lip before my hand trailed up her body to her nipple. I pinched her flesh before twisting it. Moving down her body, my teeth clamped down onto her nipple before my tongue swirled around it to soothe it.

Soon, I could feel her walls clamping down on me as she came. It didn't take long to feel my balls tighten up.

Pulling out of her, I emptied myself on the shower floor. I put her down and returned to washing myself as if nothing had happened. She was still catching her breath as she leaned against the glass shower walls.

When I finished bathing, I turned toward her and planted a kiss near her ear. "Think about that when you shower with Jacob."

Without another word, I exited the shower, allowing the door to close behind me.

Wrapping the towel around my waist, I left her by herself in the restroom and headed toward my closet choosing my usual attire. When I finished putting on my suit jacket, she walked out of the restroom with a towel wrapped around her.

I knew she was hurting from the way she walked over to the bed.

"You can leave the room when you feel better, but you need to be back by the time I'm done with business," I said before walking over to her. She smelled like me and I loved the scent on her.

"I wasn't expecting that," she muttered before lying down in my bed. A chuckle left me at the look on her face. She looked like she'd lost her favorite puppy, and it was quite humorous, as she seemed to really enjoy what we were doing moments ago.

"Does it hurt?" I asked.

I touched her bare ass, only for her to flinch in pain. It felt like her skin was heating up against my palm.

"Kiss me," I ordered.

When she didn't bother to make a move, I grabbed her and pulled her toward me. My lips met hers as her mouth opened, allowing me to explore. As her greedy tongue darted into my mouth, I slowly pulled away just to tease her.

"I'll be back, Bambolina." I smirked.

Trailing down the hall, I entered my office before shutting the door behind me. I sat down and opened a letter I had received from a worker of mine.

Suddenly, my office door opened, and my younger brother walked in. He seated himself down on the chair in front of my desk.

"When can I tell Orabella about her father?" he asked.

I noticed the looks he was giving the girl when they were together. Almost every second, he was right beside her. The way his guilt formed over his features didn't go unnoticed. I hated how lovesick he was and it only grew with each day that passed.

"Later," I muttered dismissively. If I didn't love my brother, I would have told him never. I would have said that she means absolutely nothing to him, nor should she. I couldn't understand how he could like a girl whose father was responsible for ruining our lives.

"Valentino, how long can you expect me to keep this from her?" he questioned.

"Excuse me, Vincenzo, I must've fucking stuttered so bad that you couldn't understand me. I said you will tell her *later*. Do you want to jeopardize what we've been working on our entire lives? What happened to doing this for family, huh?" I questioned.

He clenched his jaw angrily before turning to look away from me.

"One day, I'm going to be done being your cover-up. I'm going to be done with this place and *everything* involved with you. I don't even care about this damn plan, Valentino! You do! The truth is, I don't even think this is about avenging our family. This is about you making up for being a fucking coward!" Vincenzo shouted angrily before walking out of the room and slamming the door behind him.

I stared at my door for I don't know how long. Hurt enveloped me like a blanket. My own brother thought of me as some monster. My own brother who I raised with my bare hands, looked at me with hate. I let my gaze fall to my hands, where I found myself toying with a pen as his words replayed in my head over and over again.

This is about you making up for being a fucking coward.

VALENTINO

*W*e had a huge shipment coming in and I needed all of my best men to handle it. Checking my clock, I remembered how I was supposed to have a meeting with a Russian alliance of mine.

The doors opened and Adrik Zolotov walked into my office. His hair was tied back, and he was wearing his usual suit before sitting down in the chair that was waiting for him in front of my desk.

"The shipment should be there once the sun goes down. You get your weapons, I get my money," he stated before leaning back in my chair with an unbothered look on his face.

"The money is ready for you. All I need is your part of the deal," I informed him.

"Why don't you do narcotics? We can make more money that way," he wondered. His light Russian accent sometimes made it challenging to understand what he said, but after years of dealing with him—I managed to comprehend. A smirk fell on my face as I tsked.

"Drugs are messy. Weapons are easy," I explained before

getting up from my seat and walking around the desk as I buttoned the last button to my suit jacket. He stood up and nodded his head before shaking my hand.

"See you around, Valentino," Adrik stated before sliding on a pair of sunglasses. I watched him exit the office with his men following him out the door.

"One more question; what do you know about Dmitri Ivanov?" I asked, hoping he could give me more information than what I had. Adrik worked closely under Dimitri for years, it wasn't until Dimitri cut him off that Adrik began to build his own empire.

Adrik turned around and thought about it for a while, his eyebrows furrowed.

"About as much as I know about you," he stated before walking away. He snapped his fingers as he walked, signaling one of his hired men to stay put as he looked at me.

Adrik was never much of a talker. He never spoke to anyone. It took him a while to open up to me.

"Dmitri Ivanov once requested to do an alliance with our Don, Zolotov, but Zolotov immediately declined the offer. He didn't like the way Dmitri ran his business. He was too personal, and he spoke of wanting to go to war... with you," the man informed me with a curt nod.

"Thank your boss for me." I grinned.

He nodded once more, turning on his heel, and walking toward the exit.

He was desperate for more soldiers, it was obvious. The last person anyone would go to for help was Adrik Zolotov. He was an independent man, and the whole world knew it. If it weren't for the fact that my stepfather, Roberto, hadn't introduced us as kids—we wouldn't even bother speaking to one another.

Walking out of my office, I made my way to my room. The moment I was there, I opened my door and saw Anastasia sitting on the couch by the window. She looked like an angel as the sun caressed her delicate skin.

Walking over to her, I let my hand roam up her arm. It finally drew her attention, prompting her to look at me. I noticed the tears in her eyes for the first time just before she threw herself into my embrace. I instinctively wrapped around my arms her waist as she cried into the crook of my neck.

"I'm so tired of this!" she sobbed, pulling away and wiping her tears. My gaze was slightly narrowed in concern as I took her in.

"What's wrong?" I asked, hoping she was okay.

She sat down on the bed before sniffling up her tears. I reached out to move some of her hair from her face as I stood in front of her.

"I got a call from my mother's rehab facility and they told me she tried to kill herself," she whispered. I pulled her into my lap and held her to me. My hand rubbed up and down her back as she wrapped her arms around me once again.

"I know Alex didn't have a choice, but I can't shake the feeling that all anyone ever wants to do is leave. My mum has been selfish my entire life." Suddenly she stopped as realization came across her face. "I'm sorry, I tend to forget that you don't care."

She was preparing to get up, but I held onto her.

"Talk to me," I muttered.

ANASTASIA

I placed my head on his shoulder. As much as I didn't want to admit it, I loved this side of him. He made me feel like I wasn't alone at times, fostering a wish from me that he could act like that all of the time.

"All my life I have been acting like I was *her* mother. I allowed myself to have hope that, for once, she was my mum and she wanted more from herself. I understand why she's so sad. Her life is all screwed up, but is it selfish of me to wonder why she has to ruin mine?" I asked.

His hands rubbed my back soothingly again, leading to the butterflies in my stomach to suddenly awaken.

As I inhaled his cologne, I found myself growing a sudden craving for him that was more than sexual. It was hard to explain, but it was a lot harder for my mind to comprehend.

"I'm here for you, Bambolina, I just hope you remember that," he stated. His voice was deep and rich with his perfect Italian accent sliding off each word. Being held by him felt like my favorite place in the world. With Valentino, I felt protected and cared for; I felt like I was finally home.

I smiled sadly. *Was I foolish for feeling this way?*

"I was going to visit her," I whispered. He nodded his head silently, unwrapping his arms around me. I felt my heart drop at the absence of his arms. A whisk of wind hit me as the need for him to return grew drastically.

"Let's go," he declared.

I furrowed my eyebrows in confusion as I looked at him. I got off his lap, my gaze unwavering. He was so magnificent that I couldn't keep my eyes off.

He let out a sigh before running a hand through his hair. Without saying a word, I continued to follow his hand while he stood up and fixed his suit.

"You're coming?" I questioned, trying to ignore the way my heart swelled.

He ignored me and just grabbed my arm. My eyes lingered on his as he stared at me. He would do this quite often. Sometimes, I caught myself staring back and just wondering what was going through his mind.

"What?" I asked, rather bluntly.

He clenched his jaw and then began walking me out of his room. I didn't say a word.

Valentino pulled me over to his side, continuing to stroll down the hall. I just followed right beside him until we made it outside, to his car. There was no longer any energy left in my system as he pulled open the passenger side door for me to get in. Once I was seated, he walked over to the other side and got in.

No words were exchanged as he started up the car and drove down the road.

"Where am I going?" he questioned. I completely forgot to give him the address.

"Sorry," I muttered before telling him where the facility was. He seemed to know exactly where to go, so I took that as a sign to lean back in my seat. I wasn't in the mood to discuss anything, so I turned toward the window in sorrow.

I was grateful for Valentino. However, I was perplexed. Everything I felt for him was creating an unknown feeling in my heart. There were no longer any need to deny it. I could tell he cared for me as well, but he was stubborner than I was.

He turned abruptly, only to catch me staring. I quickly shifted to look outside the window. His hand came down to my thigh, where he lightly soothed my skin by rubbing up and down. It wasn't sexual, it just felt endearing.

After a moment of thinking long and hard if I should do this, I decided to just go for it. I reached down and laced my fingers with his. My head was turned toward the window looking out, so I wouldn't have to catch Valentino's expression. I knew he probably was disgusted, but I was glad he didn't pull away.

I didn't need words to know he wanted to stand by me because his actions proved everything I needed to know. Valentino allowing me to hold his hand was proof there were feelings. He wasn't the type of man to allow a woman to hold his hand. He seemed to hate romance as much as he hated when I challenged him.

Finally, I gained enough courage to look at him. His eyes met mine, a beautiful, dazzling smile danced on his lips. I could feel my heartbeat slow down.

Holding his hand meant so much more to me, and I just hoped he realized it. I broke eye contact as I decided to just look out the window for the rest of the ride. The scenery slid by as Valentino drove. I found myself loving the trees and all the nature that was showcasing its beauty.

There were no more words exchanged, but he never pulled away, either.

When we finally pulled up into the rehabilitation facility, I quickly got out. Valentino was behind me as I made my way to the front office. The receptionist already knew who I was as her face instantaneously melted from a smile into a frown.

"Miss Smith," she greeted.

I watched as she quickly logged my name onto the sign-in sheet, turning the clipboard over to me so I could sign my signature once she had done her part.

"How is Mum?" I asked as I signed my name. I was awaiting her reply, but when I didn't hear one, I looked up at her in confusion. Her eyes were on Valentino, her eyebrows rising in surprise.

"Hello?" I demanded.

She shook herself out of her daze before bringing her attention back to me. The woman better have been glad I wasn't the jealous type, or I would've been a lot ruder.

"I am so sorry, that was incredibly unprofessional of me. She's doing okay, and she has been asking about you for a while. The doctors have her under suicide watch, so she's under intense monitoring," she explained.

Her eyes moved over to Valentino briefly before quickly coming back to mine. I looked over at Valentino, who seemed busy as he talked on the phone in Italian. He sounded angry.

"Okay, thank you. Where is she?" I asked.

She ducked down to her computer screen where she began to type something into it.

With a small expression of accomplishment on her face, she glanced over at me. "Room forty-five. It's just down the hall."

"Thank you," I said, and then turned to look at Valentino once more.

The moment his eyes met mine, he hung up his phone and made his way toward me. Biting down on my lip, he placed his hand on my waist, causing that same butterfly-feeling to spread within me.

"My mum is down the hall," I told him, taking a deep breath.

He nodded his head slowly before looking over at the receptionist, who was still staring at him.

"Can I help you?" he asked her.

I turned to look at her as well, only for her to quickly look down at the computer as if she hadn't been caught gawking.

"Come on," Valentino said.

I walked with him down the hall, looking at the room numbers as we wandered. The closer we got to the number forty-five, the more nervousness seemed to seep into my mind. I didn't know what to expect. I feeling so many things, but I knew I couldn't express any of it.

Once again, my instinct that seemed mother-like, was bombarding my heart. I had to remind myself that I wasn't the parent—I was the daughter.

Finally, we reached her door. "I'll be right here," he stated. I nodded my head, pressing my lips against his cheek, and then pulling away to open the door.

The sight of my mother wasn't as bad as I had anticipated. Her arms were covered up with bandages, making me draw the conclusion she had tried to cut her wrists. I tried my best not to tear up as I walked in. Her eyes were quick to meet mine, quickly becoming glassy with tears.

"Nana!" she cried. I walked up to her and wrapped my arms around her thin frame as she cried into my shoulder. My hand rubbed up and down her back pleasingly, allowing her to let out all of her tears.

"I'm so sorry! I know I promised you. I'm sorry. Don't hate me, and don't blame yourself. I'm sorry," she sobbed.

A tear had fallen down my cheek, which I quickly wiped away. Pulling away, I nodded to let her know I understood what she was trying to say.

"I know, Mum. I don't blame you, but you can't just do this. I already lost Alex, and it was hard to get through that. I can't lose you too," I said softly.

She nodded, tears streaming as she sobbed.

"I know, Nana. I'm trying so hard to be the mother I am supposed to be. I can't," she announced, her shoulders falling in defeat as she held her head in her hands.

"Don't worry about being my mother right now. I'm doing fine and I'm happy. All I need is for you to try your best to get better. You don't need to pretend. If you feel like I'm pressuring you or something, it's okay to tell me to back off and give you a little space," I told her as my arm reached up to rub her shoulder soothingly.

She shook her head back and forth. "It's not that, Anastasia. I can't stop thinking about my little girl. How could I let her leave the world like that? How could I ever call myself a mother when I didn't give two bloody fucks that my baby had cancer?" she yelled sadly.

"Alex knew you wanted to be there with her. She talked about it all the time, and even when I told her that if you wanted to be there you would—she'd always say that the real you loved us more than anything. What's sad is that I'm talking to the *real* you right now, and I still see the exact same amount of selfishness that I saw when you were high, Mum. I know Alex is gone, but I'm still here. I'm right here!" I sobbed, tapping my chest with tears falling from my eyes.

She looked shocked, but it quickly washed away with a look of realization.

"How do you think it would make me feel to hear you killed yourself, huh? She loved you, Mum! Her last words to me were to take care of you! Why can't you see that we've always seen the good mother in you? Why can't you see what Alex has always seen—what *I* have always seen?" I yelled, the tears falling.

I knew that yelling at someone who was on the verge of suicide wasn't smart, but I kept so much bottled in, I felt the need to explode.

"You're right. I am being selfish, and I need to stop. I know I have issues, Anastasia. I know I have troubles that I need to work through. I swear to never do anything like this again if you swear to never let me get in the way of you being happy," she whispered.

I sat down on the bed, sniffling my tears, pulling her into my embrace once again. The anger I felt quickly left my body at the feeling of my mother holding onto me.

"You need to give yourself a lot more credit. Sure, things have been rocky, but you've always done your best for us, Mom," I told her.

She let out a sigh as she nodded her head softly. I wasn't sure how much time we spent hugging. After a while, our tears stopped and turned into a comforting silence.

"I know this isn't the best time, but he's here, and I feel bad leaving him out there for so long," I finally said before pulling away from the hug. Her eyebrows were pulled together in confusion before she wiped away her dried-up tears. Strolling over to the door, I pushed it open and waved my hand over for him to come into the room.

Valentino looked at me with bewilderment, yet he made his way toward me. My mother's eyes were wide and I could've sworn her jaw dropped as she looked at him.

"Mum, this is—"

"Her boyfriend. You must be Miss Olivia Smith. Anastasia has spoken so much of you," he greeted her before taking her hand and pressing it to his lips. I could've sworn I saw a blush on my mother's face. Suddenly, my mind processed his words. *Did he just call himself my boyfriend?*

"Jacob?" she asked.

My heart was hammering in my chest when he turned to

look at me. I saw the anger in his eyes that he seemed to hide so well from my mother.

"Valentino Romano," he said behind clenched teeth. "I see where Anastasia gets her beautiful looks from."

Rolling my eyes, I continued to watch the two of them. She looked over at me with approval as she smiled at Valentino.

"I'm sorry to meet you under such circumstances. Anastasia really didn't give me any notice." She chuckled and cast her gaze down.

"No, no, I didn't know I was going to be meeting you today. It's quite a surprise for me as well. I guess Anastasia just couldn't hold in her excitement of our being together. She must've wanted you to know as soon as possible." He smirked.

My mother smiled happily, and for the first time, I could see it had met her eyes. It made me glad to see that.

"Well, Mum, the doctors said we could only visit a short time. I'll be back very soon, but remember our deal," I told her before bending over and kissing the top of her head.

Just as I pulled away, Valentino grabbed onto my waist and held me against him.

"See you soon, Anastasia." She smiled. "As well as you, Valentino."

"Of course, Miss Smith. It was my pleasure meeting you," he told her.

I was quick to grab his arm and drag him out of the room. The second we closed the door, I removed myself from his hold and stormed out of the facility and over to his car.

"Are you mad?" he asked.

I narrowed my eyes at him as he unlocked the door. Before he could pull it open for me, I opened it myself. I sat down in the car and waited for him to get in, fastening my seatbelt as I did.

"Yes, very mad. Why would you lie to my mother like that?" I asked him angrily.

He scoffed sarcastically before starting up the car. "How about we talk about what's really making you mad here? Like how much you want it to be true."

"*Wow*," I drawled.

"No, what's *wow* is the fact that your mom knows about Jacob, but she doesn't know anything about me," he seethed. My eyes snapped toward him as I sent him a hard glare.

"Jealous?" I asked.

"I'll show you jealous," he angrily said, causing a chill to run down my spine.

ANASTASIA

*A*fter we got back to the mansion, he said he had some business to tend to, so he dropped me off and drove away. I was angry at our previous conversation and it only left me to truly think about what our relationship was.

Hours had passed. I'd already showered and cleaned his room a bit. When I sat down on the couch and looked out the window, I felt lost. Lying down in my lingerie gown, I stared up at the ceiling in complete silence. The room was dark, and my mind was jumping from one place to another as I just thought about everything.

The door opened, but I didn't bother to sit up. No one else dared to walk into his room, so I simply concluded that Valentino had strolled in. Slowly turning my head, I faced him, only to notice the dark bags under his eyes and the harsh yawn that left his lips.

His eyes wandered down my body before making their way back up. The bags that accessorized his eyes almost began to vanish as he walked toward me. I quickly held up my hand and shook my head. Valentino stopped like I had asked, but that didn't end the way his eyes held mine hungrily.

"I have feelings for you," I announced. Anyone could tell that he already knew that based on the way he looked at me. It made my heart break, but I had enough heartbreak to last a lifetime. At this point, I accepted it with open arms. No longer did heartbreak make me want to cry and scream. There was so much of it that I was suffocating. Adding on more didn't do any more damage than what had already been done. "I understand you don't feel the same way—which is fine because I can't force you to. I just wanted to let you know the reason why I can't do this anymore. I'd like to think of myself as a strong, beautiful, smart woman, and I deserve someone who wants every part of that, not just my body. So, with that said, thank you for a lot, Mr. Romano, but I'm leaving this job and this place." I stood up and walked toward the door, staying as emotionless as he could be.

As I walked past him, he grabbed onto my wrist and pulled me toward his chest. My eyes moved away from his because I knew I would get sucked into this whirlpool of feelings I had for him.

"Anastasia," he said. I finally looked up into his eyes and automatically wished that I hadn't. His eyes were so beautiful, they glowed brightly as he looked down at me.

"I want you here with me. You wouldn't be here if I didn't want you," he finished. I bit down onto my lip before shaking my head. There was a sadness that wanted to come out. Everything in me wanted to be right there, but I couldn't.

"I was a virgin before I met you. My life isn't just sex like your life is. I want to have conversations and talk about dumb nothings. I even want to argue about things and laugh. It's not fair to ask that of you because I *know* you, Valentino. You don't do that kind of thing," I explained. He looked away momentarily with a clenched jaw.

"What are you saying—you want a relationship? I've never been in a relationship," he stated. I let out a loud exhale. *That's exactly what I wanted.* I wanted him wholeheartedly, but I knew I couldn't have him. Everything good in life got snatched away eventually, it wouldn't be such a crime to push this one away before it's given the chance.

He must've seen the defeat in my face because his other hand was quick to pull me closer. "I could try," Valentino muttered.

I turned his face to look at me. Even though he said it, I still wasn't sure if it was my imagination. The big bad Valentino just said that he could try to be in a relationship for *me*.

"Why?" I questioned, shocked. He gazed down at me. His eyes pierced through mine as a thought ran across his face.

Then, he leaned down and pressed his lips against mine. My body felt like it was melting against him as his arms curled around my waist and pulled me in even closer. His tongue massaged mine tenderly. I had to keep myself from touching him as he continued to kiss me.

I began to move my mouth against his as my hands wandered up to his hair. His mouth was dominating our kiss, leaving me to only follow. Slowly, he pulled away with his eyes on my lips. When his eyes flashed up to meet mine, I could feel a pool between my legs. I hated the way he made me feel.

"Stay," he whispered before pecking my lips. His lips hovered over mine as he glanced up into my eyes, pressing his lips against mine for a longer amount of time soon after. "Stay for me."

When he pulled away, I watched him look around the room.

"Thank you for cleaning my mess, Bambolina," he told me. I didn't know what to say, but he settled for kissing me one more time—only this time it was on my cheek. Then, I watched him walk into the restroom and turn on the shower.

As I stood there, I didn't know what to do. I really wanted to stay, but I couldn't knock off the feeling of whether or not I could trust his word. He said he could try, but I couldn't picture Valentino skipping off into the sunset with me, hand-in-hand. Maybe if he could try to be what I wanted, I could try as well.

Deciding to just give him a chance, I pulled back the duvet cover and laid down. His smell was quick to consume me as soon as I tucked myself in.

Every time I closed my eyes, I tried to picture what my life would've been like without Valentino. I probably wouldn't have ever been able to pay off my debt or put my mother in rehab. In some ways, he had made my life better.

After some time, I decided to just let myself fall asleep. My eyes shut, but the sound of the shower turning off made me alert with anticipation. Moments after that, the door opened, and I could feel Valentino walking toward the bed and lying down. He pulled me into his chest like he always managed to do.

It brought a small smile to my face as he ran his hand through my hair. "Goodnight, beautiful," he whispered.

My body was quick to fall asleep after that. There was a warmth in my heart as I hugged his muscular frame.

ANASTASIA

When I woke up, Valentino was already getting dressed for the day. I couldn't help but sigh as I watched him. He was such a handsome man. As I looked at him, I tried to find any flaw, but I came up empty-handed every time. From his black hair to his strong jaw and beautiful blue eyes, I used to dream of finding a man like him.

"I actually wanted to talk about you for once. I noticed we always talk about me, but I would really love to even the playing field a bit," I muttered sadly as he threw on one of his shirts.

He walked over to me and stood by the edge of the bed. My knees sank into the mattress as I sat up and began to button up his plain white shirt while he just stared down at me. When I glanced into his eyes, he leaned down and pecked my lips. A warmth spread throughout my body and hugged me tightly as a small smile made its way onto my face.

"We can talk later, *no?*" he asked.

I let out a huff of air before shrugging and throwing myself down onto his bed where I pulled the blanket over my head. When a groan left his lips, I couldn't help but grin. Turning around, I quickly replaced my smile with a frown to continue my act. His arms wrapped around my waist as he pulled me into his chest.

"I don't like to talk," Valentino stated. I wrapped my arms around him in response, before resting my head on his chest. I knew he didn't like to open up, but I felt it would help me connect with him more. I didn't know much about him except for the fact that he may or may not kill people, he owns a club, and his half-brother is the Don of a mafia.

"I had a mother. Her name was Agnella, and she was the best woman I had ever met. Her heart was so big that she cared too much about everyone else and didn't see when she needed care herself. She was the first person I ever loved—no one was like my mother. Not even my *bitch of a father* could match to how much I looked up to that woman," he explained.

It was exactly how I felt about Alex.

"What's your favorite memory of her?" I asked. *That* was the question I wished people would ask instead of how I was doing. I didn't want to know how sorry they were because of her death, I wanted to know that they actually cared enough to learn about her.

"I was with my brother, Vincenzo. We were down by this lake that was near our house and I told my brother that one time I caught a fish with my bare hands. I never did, but he believed me. It was understandable, seeing as he couldn't say anything other than '*papa*' and '*mama*.' My mother had finished dressing us up to '*perfezione*' since my stepfather said that was the way men were supposed to dress all the time. So, Enzo was in this nice suit. His hair was combed, and he was wearing these expensive shoes Roberto, my stepfather, had bought him. Enzo always wanted to be better than me, so he walked into the shallow part of the lake and he tried to catch a fish." He laughed. An actual smile made its way onto his face and it was beautiful. It was so contagious that I wished he would smile more.

"My mama was so mad when he walked into the house drenched in stinky lake water. His father, Roberto, was just sitting on the couch, shaking his head. Mama looked at me and we all just started laughing. Keep in mind that Enzo was just a baby." He smiled. I bit down onto my lip as my smile only seemed to grow.

Getting on my tippy toes, I grabbed his face gently between my hands and pecked his lips.

"I love, um, I love that you're talking to me," I whispered.

Closing my eyes tightly, I could only hope he didn't notice my *almost* slip up. I also couldn't believe that I had just almost said '*I love you*' to him.

When I opened my eyes, he was staring at me. I watched as his smile disappeared. He turned to look away from me before nodding his head awkwardly.

"I have to go," he muttered. My eyes shut as soon as he leaned down and kissed my cheek. At the sound of the door closing, they opened. He knew exactly what I had *almost* said to him. It was in my eyes and everywhere on my face. I loved Valentino Romano and I hated it.

A frown came across my face as I sat down and stared at absolutely nothing. Deep down, I knew he would never love me back.

ANASTASIA

$\mathcal{I}$ regretted that day in his room more than anything. I hadn't seen Valentino in a whole week. For the first three days, I decided to sleep in his room and just hope he would show up. He never did. Not even when it was nighttime. It made me wonder if he were with someone else. The thought broke my heart so much that I stopped sleeping in his room and returned to mine.

I had never felt so alone. I couldn't count how many times I cried and wondered why my life had to be so complicated. No matter what I did, I could not be content. Even when I tried to text Jacob about dog-sitting Max like I was supposed to, I couldn't get a response.

Deciding that today would be the last day of drowning in a pit of my own sadness, I would get dressed and do something productive. I got up and made my way to the bathroom. I took a shower, brushed my teeth, and did everything else for good personal hygiene.

After I finished, I wrapped a towel around myself and went to my closet. All of my clothes were either short or tight. With a sigh, I put on my trademark pink lingerie before slipping on a pair of shorts and a pink crop top. Then, I slipped on a pair of socks, since it wasn't like I had any place else to be other than the mansion.

As soon as I finished, the door opened, and Valerio walked in. I couldn't help but smile as I shuffled over and embraced him in a hug. I hadn't seen him since Valentino said I was basically suspended from going into the club.

"How you been, Barbie doll?" he asked, a big smile on his face. I pulled away from the hug with a sad smile.

"As good as I can get," I responded.

"When are you coming back to the club?" he questioned. I could only shrug my shoulders as I thought about how I was going to pay my rent if I weren't getting paid. There was also the fact that I had to pay the monthly bill to the rehab facility for my mother.

"I'm not sure. I've been thinking about finding a job somewhere else. This place is just becoming too personal," I explained. He nodded his head slowly, a sad look on his face.

"Are you going to keep living here? I'm sure Mr. Romano wouldn't mind," he said. I was almost completely sure he *would* mind. Shaking my head, I gave him one more sad smile.

"No. I'll probably get an apartment somewhere until my mother gets better," I answered. He opened his arms once more, leaving me to walk into them. His hugs were always so brotherly, and it made me happy.

"Is he here?" I asked him.

He shook his head. "No. He's been gone for a few hours now."

As soon as we pulled away, he opened my bedroom door for me. I gave him one last smile before walking out of my room and down the hall. We said our goodbyes before heading off in different ways

Just then, my phone began to ring. After pressing accept, I

held it to my ear and waited for the person on the other line to speak.

"Anastasia?" Jacob questioned. A large breath of relief came through me at the sound of his voice. It had felt like I hadn't heard from him in so long.

"Jacob, I have missed you so much. What happened?" I asked. He went on to explain how he didn't want to talk over the phone and how he was outside of the mansion.

My brows pulled together when I headed to the front door. When I saw his car outside, I strolled over to it and got into the passenger seat.

"What's up?" I wondered.

"Do you know a man by the name of Romano?" I let out a loud sigh, already gaining a feeling of where this conversation was heading. It was something bad, and I knew it. "He threatened me to stay away from you. Are you with that man, Anastasia?"

"No, not technically," I murmured.

"I'm worried about you. He seems dangerous, and I don't understand how you can choose a guy like him over me. I would do anything for you, don't you know that?" I gulped before allowing my eyes to cast down to my lap. It was the conversation I was trying to avoid so I could keep him as my friend.

He was right about one thing. How could I choose a man like Valentino over Jacob, who wasn't stubborn, and who seemed like he knew how to love a woman. Jacob was more emotionally available than Valentino would ever be, yet Valentino owned my heart.

"Please, just give me a chance. I promise I will treat you the way you deserve to be treated, which will be many times better than that Romano guy ever could," Jacob let out. I opened my mouth to speak, but before a word could get out, Jacob pressed his lips to mine.

I was shocked. I didn't know what to say or do without losing our friendship, so I just sat there. There were no shocks or tingles like I got with Valentino, all I felt was lips moving against mine until they weren't anymore.

Jacob's car door was harshly jerked open before he was snatched out of his own vehicle. My jaw dropped to see Valentino slamming his fist into Jacob's face. I hurriedly got out of the car, screaming in protest for Valentino to stop.

He completely ignored me and continued to pummel Jacob's face. At first, Jacob was fighting back, but he soon looked like a ragdoll as he laid there, accepting his defeat.

I ran over to Valentino and tried my best to push him off Jacob, but he wouldn't budge. Blood was spilling out of Jacob's nose and mouth as Valentino beat him to the pulp.

It wasn't until he stopped that he finally looked at me. His breath was uneven, and his eyes were full of rage. Then, he turned back to look at Jacob, who was coughing up blood.

"Get up and get the hell off my property! If I see you near her again, I won't hesitate to fucking kill you! Consider this my last warning!" Valentino seethed before grabbing my arm in his firm hold. I looked back at Jacob, worry coursing through me. He was trying to get up, but ended up falling back down to the ground again.

Valentino dragged me into the house where he led me to his bedroom. Even then, he didn't bother to let go.

"What are you trying to do, huh? Get back at me for not talking to you?" he yelled, fury still evident on his feautures.

I sniffled as I thought about poor Jacob. He shouldn't have kissed me, but Valentino shouldn't have hit him. Jacob had done so much for me, and I hated that he got a whiff of my bad luck and ended up beaten for a girl he really liked.

"No, I'm not a child. Jacob called me and said he needed to speak to me, so I went out there and he kissed me, but it's not like you deserve some explanation. Just because you put some claim on me doesn't mean I belong to you. I am allowed to do as I please, and you need to respect that just like how I respect it when you decide to do it!" I declared. "You avoided me for a week like a teenager just because I almost said that I loved you. I would've understood if you told me you didn't feel the same way, but you left. That's what you do—you use me and then you *leave*. I can't handle having any more of this drama. I have had enough to last a long time."

"Why do you assume that I use you?" he questioned, frustration beaming on my face. "I want you in ways that I never wanted anyone else, and I'm not talking about sex. You don't understand why it's so hard for me to love you like you want me to love you."

"Then help me understand," I insisted.

"*I* don't even understand, but I know that I have feelings for you, too, Anastasia. Seeing you with Jacob killed me," he said, his voice growing softer with each word.

I sighed before wrapping my arms around him. "I'm here, always."

ANASTASIA

After a while of being lost in our thoughts with one another, he received a phone call. I watched him pace around the room, rubbing the bridge of his nose in frustration.

"I told you I'll be there," he angrily said into the phone before walking over to my side of the bed and pressing his lips to mine. I found myself never wanting him to leave. I immediately responded by wrapping my arms around his neck in an attempt to not let him go.

"Shut up, Vincenzo. I'll be there," Valentino growled into the phone before hanging up. He pushed the blanket away from me and immediately grabbed onto my boob. His lips were quick to meet mine. I moaned as my hand wandered down to the button of his slacks.

"I have to go, Bambolina. I'll be home soon, and I want you back in my room, *no?*" he stated before pulling away. He got me all hot and bothered on purpose, just to leave me hanging. Valentino probably thought it was humorous, but if only he knew it was far from that.

He pecked my lips. "See you soon."

I could only watch as he walked out. Boredom loomed in every corner of the room. I found myself strolling around nosily as I looked through all of Valentino's clothes and belongings.

With a sigh, I bent down and grabbed a pair of shorts. Valentino left his button-down shirt on the floor, so I took it upon myself to place it on. I loved the elegant smell of Valentino's cologne. It made it easier to imagine his arms still wrapped around me.

Without a second thought, I headed over to the kitchen. The shirt almost reached my knees, but it was exactly what I loved about it.

When I entered the kitchen, I immediately noticed Orabella. She looked a lot calmer than she did the day I first met her.

Just as I was about to speak to her, the Don walked in. I watched as they seated themselves in the living room. It wasn't difficult to pick up on the way the Don looked into her eyes. Anyone could easily see all of the adoration he had for her. I even enjoyed how he made it so visible. He had no shame in the world knowing how much he cared for her. I only wished Valentino were more like that.

"Will you please go tell Orabella that the food is ready?" Sarah asked me. I nodded in response.

"Never," I could hear Orabella, leaning up to plant a kiss on his lips before hiding her face back into the crook of his neck. I was envious of them. It was everything I wanted, but it seemed like only a dream for me—a *fairytale*.

"Food is ready," I said, walking in with a proud smile on my face. Orabella smiled sweetly which I followed with a wink. The Don's eyes met mine, so I quickly walked back into the kitchen. He was scary. I think the most frightening part about him was his tattoos everywhere on his skin.

Suddenly, my gaze traveled over to the door to see

Valentino walk in. I followed his stare as he observed his brother and Orabella. I could see his jaw clenching along with his clenched fists. My brows pulled together as I wondered what could possibly be going through his mind.

There was something I didn't know about and I could just feel it. I remember how angry Valentino got when I almost left the house with Orabella, and how he seemed ready to murder his brother just now. My shoulders fell as I looked between Orabella and Valentino. I hoped nothing ever happened between them intimately.

Shaking my head, I decided to just let it go.

I was studying Valentino's every move even as he began searching around the room until his eyes met mine. I noticed the smirk on his face once he noticed me. My eyebrow arched in question before I walked toward him.

"You're wearing my shirt," he said as his hand played with the button. Nodding my head, I looked down at it before raising my head back up to look into his eyes.

"It still smells like you." I smiled innocently.

He chuckled before kissing my cheek, and then surprising me by continuing to plant kisses down my jawline. His arm circled around my waist as I could feel his tongue caress my skin.

Without warning, Vincenzo cleared his throat, leaving Valentino to pull away. Orabella giggled as my cheeks coated a light pink. Valentino rolled his eyes at his brother, leaving me a light chuckle to escape my lips. They acted like such normal siblings despite being the kings of organized crime.

"Have you eaten?" Valentino asked me. I shook my head when suddenly the loud sound of my stomach growling interrupted us.

"Good. Come with me," Valentino ordered.

"Where? Should I get dressed?" I questioned. He smirked,

grabbing onto my hand and basically dragging me out of the house and to his car.

The second we were in his vehicle, he grabbed me by my neck and pressed his lips against mine. He was kissing me like his life depended on it, and I'd be a liar to say it didn't turn me on. My ability to not catch up made him groan as his tongue darted into my mouth.

Pulling away, he bit down on my lip, tugging at it. "I've been wanting to do that since I walked in." He chuckled. I couldn't help the smile that tugged on my lips at the sound of his words.

His hand came down to my thigh as he pulled out of the driveway. The huge smile never left my lips as I watched his beautiful face concentrate on the road.

ANASTASIA

The car was parked in the middle of nowhere. There was nothing but trees and birds that called out from above us. The rich scent of woods clogged my nostrils as I opened the door and stepped out. I couldn't hide my smile as I looked around me—it was beautiful.

When I turned to face Valentino, who had already gotten out of the car, his eyes were glued on me. My smile seemed to grow as I looked at him before staring up above me at the beautiful sight of green and sky. The wind whisked through my hair, embracing me in nature's hug. I loved the outdoors.

"This isn't all, Bambolina," he said. My eyebrow rose as he locked his door before walking up to me. I decided to follow his lead with his arm curled around my waist. We walked and walked. I distracted myself with the animals that ran by. The place was lovely, and I could only question why I had never ventured out into the wild before. The silence Valentino and I shared was nurturing. I found myself gaining comfort in the musical quietness.

After what felt like half a mile, we made it to a huge restaurant that sat right in the middle of nowhere. My gaze strayed over the elegance of it all. It was made entirely of wood and the light had a warm glow to it, causing it to look like a large, cozy home.

A woman walked out of the restaurant wearing a beautiful red gown and the man beside her was dressed in a suit. Luckily, Valentino was wearing a suit, as opposed to me, who wasn't wearing anything other than a pair of shorts and a huge button-down shirt.

"You didn't tell me it was a date. I even mentioned changing my clothes, but you didn't give me the chance to." I pouted. We stopped walking, and he took the time to peer down at my figure. A smirk plastered itself onto his face. Pushing his sunglasses to the top of my head, he gave me a small kiss on my cheek.

"You look sexy like this. Plus, we aren't eating in there—we're eating in *there*," he said, pointing toward a few cabins that sat right beside the restaurant. I noticed how some waiters and waitresses would walk from the restaurant to the cabins with a tray of food in their hands. My stomach growled at the sight.

We began to head toward the cabins. As we walked, my hand moved over to his that lay comfortably on my waist. I grabbed his hand before he could protest and interlocked our fingers together. It always made me happy to do intimate couple-like things with him.

Once we made it to the cabin, the door was opened for the both of us. A waiter nodded as Valentino walked by. As soon as I strolled in, my jaw literally dropped. There were rose petals everywhere that led to a beautifully decorated table. Everything was so romantic; it was exactly what I wanted. As I I looked over the entire cabin, my smile grew. It looked a lot bigger on the inside than the outside.

I couldn't stop myself from looking into the bedroom—which had candles all around the bed frame, along with roses on top of the bedding. Everything was so perfect and romantic, which was very unlike Valentino.

The waiter pulled out a chair for me while Valentino sat down right across from me at the very small table.

"My name is Ferdinand, and this is Alissa. We will be serving you both today," the waiter introduced. I smiled kindly at him before my eyes moved over to the waitress, who must've been waiting for our arrival. She looked down at my clothing with disapproval before glancing over at Valentino. Her gaze stayed there for a long moment.

"Hi, Ferdinand. Hi, Alissa. My name is Anastasia." I introduced myself, holding my hand out for them to shake. Ferdinand looked shocked, but he shook my hand anyway. Alissa shook my hand as well, but with a roll of her eyes.

"You're a kind woman, Miss Anastasia. Most people who come here don't do that," he stated. A smile graced my lips which he happily returned. With one last curt nod, Ferdinand walked out of the cabin with Alissa right behind him.

I couldn't see why anyone wouldn't be kind enough to introduce themselves back. I thought it was a part of American custom.

"You know, I've never actually been served at a restaurant before. It was always me who did the serving. It's kind of strange," I stated randomly. I glanced over at Valentino, who had been staring at me intensely. He leaned back in his chair with his eyes still burning into mine.

"Well, I will take you out more often," he declared. A smile crossed my face as I looked at him. Butterflies in my stomach began to cheer at his declaration.

"This is just our first date, and you're already planning a second one? That's a little creepy," I teased, picking up a menu. He chuckled lightly. I could still feel him staring at me, but I decided to just ignore it.

"What will we be drinking?" I asked to fill the silence in

the room. While skimming through the menu, I couldn't help but look at the very expensive prices. The room must've cost a fortune, along with our own private waiter and waitress. It felt good knowing he was willing to go to such great lengths to make me happy.

"I don't know about you, but I know exactly what I'll be drinking," he stated seductively. I slowly glanced over at him to see the dark glint in his eyes.

"And what's that?" I questioned with a raised brow. He smirked at my response, his eyes lowering to my breast. I suddenly realized that my top buttons were undone, leaving my breast almost completely bare.

"You," he let out. I rolled my eyes playfully at him before placing the menu on the table just as Alissa walked in. Based on the way her eyes trained on Valentino, I knew she was about to flirt. Allowing her to do what she had to do, I picked up my menu and looked through it once more.

"Anything I could get you to drink?" she asked lowly, her voice growing a little husky. Behind the menu, I peeked up to see her twirling her hair as she looked at him. He glanced over at her, leaving me to look right back down at the menu.

"Wine. Both of us," he ordered nonchalantly. I placed my menu down to see her staring at him while he had been staring at me. She was acting as if I weren't there.

"Coming right up, sir," she gritted out. I laughed lightly to myself, watching her turn around and stiffly move her hips as she walked. The girls at the club would be laughing at her if they saw the act she was attempting to pull.

"I like that most about you," he said randomly. My eyes snapped over to look into his as my eyebrows rose in question.

"Other than your happiness despite everything bad, forgiveness, confidence, and the way you're not scared to speak your mind. I like how you are so kind to the point you can't even allow yourself to be jealous," he pointed out. I processed his words and felt myself falling into deep thought.

"Are you talking about Alissa?" I asked. He nodded his head slowly.

"I don't get jealous because I understand why women stare and flirt with you. You are a very attractive man. If I were them, I would stare too. Would I flirt when there is a woman in front of you? No, of course not, because it's rude. Although, a lot of insecure women feel the need to act confident. She's just an unhappy girl looking to make me feel just as bad as she does. I don't blame her," I explained.

"People take advantage of people who think like that, Bambolina," he said. I nodded, thinking about my mum and the countless times she had stolen from me.

"I know. Good thing I have you," I whispered. He bit down on his lip before looking off, giving me the perfect view of his jawline. Just in time, Alissa walked back in with a bottle of wine. She poured wine into my empty glass.

I smiled brightly at her. "Thank you, Miss Alissa."

She gave me a small smile before pouring wine into Valentino's glass as well. He watched me with a smirk on his face, shaking his head.

"What?" I asked just as she left the cabin. For the first time, I noticed the soft sound of classical music.

"Nothing," he muttered.

"Good evening to you both. Have you decided what you will be having?" Ferdinand asked, suddenly making an appearance. I still didn't know what to eat, so I just turned to look at Valentino, hoping he would get the message that I wanted him to decide for me.

"We will have Tuscan tomato bread soup with steamed mussels, and beef brasato with pappardelle and mint," he ordered. Ferdinand didn't say anything in response, so out of curiosity, I glanced up at him. His eyes were staring deep into my almost completely exposed breast.

Rolling my eyes, I buttoned up the top. I had completely forgotten about it.

"Will I have to give Matteo a call about his staff? *Take our order, get out, and bring new people,*" Valentino demanded angrily. I had no clue what he said but based on the way Ferdinand ran out of the room, I could only assume it wasn't kind.

"I want to learn Italian," I muttered.

Valentino chuckled to himself, the agitation he showed quickly disappearing. He stood up from his chair, leaving it to squeal against the flooring, and he held out his hand for me. Glancing at his open palm, a smile crept onto my face as I placed my hand in his. He was quick to pull me up with his hand around my waist and my breast against his chest. A gasp escaped me as my head instinctively landed on his shoulder. My cheeks were beginning to hurt from smiling so much.

"I can't dance," I informed him. He only chuckled, moving me with him to the light sound of music. I couldn't stop the quickness of my heart. For a moment, I could almost feel his heartbeat racing as well. I wondered if I made him just as nervous as he made me..

"You're dancing," he replied, stating the obvious. Then, he dipped me, causing me to erupt in a fit of laughter as one of my legs latched at his waist. When he pulled me back up, he spun me around until my back hit his chest. I haven't felt so happy in so long. Valentino made the bad luck that always stood in as my shadow, easily disappear. He may be a scary, dangerous man, but he was my savior. My life without him would be a deep pit of darkness.

He gave my neck a small kiss before whisking me back around. I lowered my head down on his shoulder as his hands returned to my waist. We continued to sway to the music, loving each other's embrace.

His fingertips trailed down to my bottom, where he moved up the shirt and gripped my ass. I couldn't help but let out a giggle.

"Thank you for this," I told him. Pulling my head up from his shoulder, I gazed into his eyes. I grabbed ahold of his face and stood on my tippy-toes to kiss his lips. He promised me he would try, and I was loving the effort.

"You deserve the world," he muttered as he grabbed my hands away from his face and leaned down to peck my lips.

"Teach me Italian." I repeated my wishes from earlier.

"I like the idea of you not knowing what I am saying," he stated with a smirk full of mischief dancing on his lips. Narrowing my eyes at him, I tried my best to be upset, but the smile on my face just wouldn't falter. *I'll just learn Italian in secret.*

At that moment, a man entered the room with a nice fancy white suit and a tray of food in his hands. The moment Valentino looked over at him, a huge smile broke out on his face. It was so genuine and contagious, it made me happy.

"Valentino!" He exclaimed just before placing the tray of food on our table. The man smiled brightly at me as he looked between me and Valentino.

"Who is this?" he asked Valentino. I could see the look of pride on his face. I turned to look at Valentino, waiting for him to introduce us.

"Anastasia, this is the man I've known since I was a child, Matteo," Valentino introduced. I smiled at him, sticking my hand out for him to shake. He completely ignored it and embraced me in a hug. My mind processed his words as I realized Valentino had mentioned a Matteo before. I wondered if he owned the restaurant.

"Gorgeous, gorgeous girl! It makes me happy seeing

Valentino actually out with a girl for once." He chuckled. I looked over at Valentino as he pulled away from the hug. As soon as Matteo broke the hug, Valentino wrapped his arm around my waist.

"Well, I'll let you get back to your *tempo da solo*. See you soon, Valentino," he said. I watched Valentino nod his head before Matteo walked up to me and grabbed a hold of my hand. He planted his cool lips against my knuckles before rubbing the spot soothingly.

"Come by anytime you want, Miss Anastasia." He smiled. I returned the smile happily just before he turned around and walked out of the cabin, shutting the door as he left. He seemed so sweet.

"I'm starving," I groaned as the sweet aroma of the food filled my nostrils. Sitting back down, I grabbed the plate of pasta with some other stuff on top that looked incredibly delicious.

I didn't want to be rude, so I waited for Valentino to be seated. Just as he sat down, I grabbed the fork and began to dig right in. The food was absolutely delicious.

"Does that man own this restaurant?" I asked. Valentino nodded slowly.

The restaurant was perfect, and I loved the idea of the cabins. It set the perfect mood that I couldn't help but fall in love with.

"Yes, I helped him start this business. I met him when I was a young boy and he helped me sometimes with Enzo. I've always been grateful to him, so when he told me about his dream with this place—I assisted," he explained. I nodded as a warmth spread throughout my heart. He was such a good man even if he never showed it.

"I've always wondered; how is it that *you* took care of Vincenzo, but *he's* the Don and not you?" I asked, taking another forkful of the noodles and stuffing it in my mouth.

That question seemed to have really gotten his attention because his eyes strayed off.

"Let me ask you something," he began.

I set my fork down and gave him my undivided attention.

"If you were given the choice of your life or mine, tell me, would you die for me?" he asked

"Yes, I would," I answered with no hesitation. "I told you that I love you."

He smiled, but it slowly went away, letting me know that he was about to say something serious.

"The Don isn't my brother," he explained. My eyebrows came together. I couldn't stop the tilt of my head as I looked at him. *If the Don wasn't Vincenzo, then that must mean...*

"You're the Don?" I asked, my jaw dropping slightly. This whole time I had been scared of Vincenzo when I should've actually been scared of Valentino.

"Is there anything else I should know?" I asked.

"You say you love me. Soon, you won't," he muttered. My eyebrows grew furrowed as I stared at him. I didn't like the words that came out of his mouth, and I could only hope that they weren't true.

ANASTASIA

After eating, a new waiter walked into the cabin to grab our dishes, bowing a goodbye once he finished. I watched him earnestly as he turned on his heel and walked out of the cabin, leaving Valentino and I completely alone. I watched as he just stared at me. The atmosphere fogged up with sexual tension.

"Come here," he finally said. I stood up from the chair and walked over to him. Valentino pulled his chair out slightly. His eyes dropped from my eyes to my breasts just before traveling down to my waist. Being under his heated gaze left me aroused.

My exhilaration only increased when his hand crept underneath the white shirt when he pulled me onto his lap. He smelled so good, and I was loving every inhale.

His hand ran through my hair before he grabbed a handful of my strands and craned my neck back, so I was vulnerable to him. I could feel my bottom right on top of his semi-erect cock. His other hand curled around my waist, pulling me in closer.

I made sure to move my hips against him just to turn him

on even more. His hands traveled up my waist to my breasts where he tore the shirt open, leaving a few buttons to fly everywhere. With my breasts now bare, he fondled them, making my eyes roll back.

"The cabin is ours for the night," he whispered into my ear as my eyes shut. I couldn't take it anymore. I straddled his waist before placing my lips aggressively against his. He immediately responded, encouraging me to push away his suit jacket.

"Take it off," I moaned against his lips, growing irritated with his jacket. He chuckled softly before removing it. Suddenly, he erupted in laughter. I frowned. I couldn't figure out what was so funny.

"Are you laughing at me?" I pouted, breaking our kiss once more. He shrugged his shoulders with a grin on his face before leaning back.

"You are quite aggressive when you're horny," he observed. I rolled my eyes and stood up. Pulling my shirt together with my hand, I held it there to keep him from seeing my bare upper-half.

"You're worse," I let out.

My embarrassment could be seen as heat crept up to my cheeks. Turning around, I headed toward the door, but I was stopped when he grabbed my arm. I wasn't sure if it was his intention to make fun of me, but it felt like it.

"I never said I didn't enjoy it, Bambolina," he stated. I was no longer in the mood for him, so I just turned back around to walk away, but his hand on my arm wouldn't allow me to. Letting out a sigh, I looked into his eyes to see that the playful spark he was sporting earlier had evaporated.

"Do you have a condom?" I asked randomly. His expression was quickly replaced with one of mock of a frown. I narrowed my eyes as I watched him. Whatever he was about to say, I knew that he would not mean any of it.

"I completely forgot to bring one. That really sucks, but we can still have fun." He smirked before leaning down to kiss me. I wrapped my arm around his neck just before I broke the kiss.

"No condom, no sex," I whispered into his ear seductively. He pulled away from me with furrowed brows.

"What did you just say?" he asked. I shook my head back and forth before hurrying into the bedroom and locking the door behind me.

Valentino was fast, seeing as I soon heard him wiggling the doorknob and knocking on the door.

Laughter filled the room as I allowed myself to make fun of him now. It was very important to me that I return the exact same treatment he had done to me. I knew one day I would be able to get my revenge from the time he left me hanging a few mornings ago.

"It's like that?" he asked. I only smiled at his words before the sound of him walking away could be heard from outside the door.

Moments passed and I no longer heard anything, so I took that as a sign that he left to give me some alone time.

There were no clothes for me to wear, but I knew that I should probably take a bath. Shrugging my shoulders, I walked into the adjoining bathroom and let the water run.

The restroom looked just as romantic as every other room in the cabin. There were lit candles, wine by the tub, and even roses all around it. Plus, the dim lighting only added to the romantic appeal.

All of a sudden, I felt bad for Valentino. He had brought me here and I locked him out of his own room. Maybe I would let him in after my bath.

Taking off the torn-up shirt, I slipped out of my shorts. I had to bend over to remove my slippers from my feet. Once I was ready and the tub was full, I turned the water off and climbed in. The hot water coaxed my muscles into instant relaxation. My eyes quickly shut as I leaned back, letting the water work its magic.

"You're enjoying a bath without me? How heartless of you," Valentino suddenly said. My eyes snapped open as I gazed at the beautiful man before me. He was taking off his shirt, displaying his every muscle.

"How did you get in?" I asked, letting the worry drip from my words as he unbuttoned his pants. His body was perfect, and his muscles flexed with every move he seemed to make.

"I have my ways," he alluded. Valentino pulled down his boxers, giving me a perfect view. I couldn't help but stare in amazement. He was huge, sexy, and all mine.

Slowly, my gaze trailed up his body to his beautiful eyes as a smirk made its way onto his face. Biting down on my lip, I watched him get into the tub right behind me. Since he was a giant, it took a lot of moving around on my part until I rested perfectly, right on top of him.

"I was going to let you in after I finished my bath," I told him. He didn't say anything. He kissed my jawline and trailed down my neck. I giggled slightly at how it tickled. That didn't seem to stop him at all, he just continued to move his lips expertly against my skin. He always knew exactly what to do in order to get me aroused.

Turning over, I wrapped my arms around his neck once more. My lips met his, and his tongue was quick to massage mine. I could feel his growing erection against me, leaving me more excited as we kissed. His hand pulled my ass closer, so I was pressed up against his cock. I began to grind against his length, loving the feel of him against me.

"Stand up and turn around," he said. I did as told and leaned forward with my hands against the wall. He ran his hand up and down my clit, and then inserted a finger, working it in a circular motion, massaging my walls. He inserted another finger, and then a third, continuing to work my hole until there was little resistance. I thrust my hips, meeting his fingers each time they thrust into me, fucking myself with his fingers.

He pulled his fingers out and moved between my legs. I could feel the tip of his head against my cunt, pressing only slightly. He probed me with just the tip, then the head pushed in. I moaned as the edge of his large cock passed the entrance.

He grabbed my hips and started stroking in and out of me, going a little deeper with each stroke. I slightly rocked my hips, encouraging him to go deeper. Finally, with one firm stroke, he penetrated fully, slapping his balls against me. I moved my hips in a circular motion, tightened slightly, and milked his throbbing shaft. He held still and let me do the work for the moment.

As I rocked my hips and pulled him in and out of me, he grabbed my breasts and started fucking me. He began slowly, picking up the pace as he went, repeatedly pulling nearly all the way out, and then burying his shaft to full depth. My moans turned to murmurs of, "It feels so good. Keep going. Don't stop."

He pinched my nipple bud while his lips went over to my neck. I could feel him sucking against my skin as his cock slid in and out of my folds.

"*I love it when I am inside of you,*" he groaned as his hands slid down from my breasts to my ass, where he squeezed my flesh. A moan climbed out of me once again as soon as his finger came down to toy with my clit. My body shuddered and I knew I was close.

"Say that again," I moaned. Even though I had no clue what he said, it sounded completely sexy coming from his mouth.

"*Come for me, baby,*" he said between thrusts. My head fell back once again as he rubbed my clit up and down, and then in circular motions. My body felt like it was tingling, and my head was on fire as pleasure coaxed my veins.

Finally, I could feel myself coming. "Fuck!" I moaned as my body shuddered against him. His hand came up to my neck, where he held me against him, while he sped up his thrusting in and out of me. Suddenly, he let out a quiet grunt before coming.

"Did you just come inside me?" I questioned. He only turned on the shower in response as the bathwater funneled down the drain. He completely ignored my question and just stood underneath the water as it sprayed through his hair. I watched his strong arms move up to use his fingers to comb through the jet-black strands. He looked like a model, especially when his piercing eyes met mine.

"Am I talking to myself, Valentino?" I asked. I could still feel his cum leaking out of me. It was beginning to piss me off that he just completely ignored me.

"Fine, whatever," I said, ready to step out of the shower. He grabbed me by my waist and placed me in front of him. Letting out a sigh, I looked at him as he stared down at me.

"I didn't mean to, but at the same time, I kind of did," he whispered into my ear before his teeth tugged at my earlobe. A chill ran down my spine at his words, and I found myself relaxing within his hold. I knew that the minute I got home I would take one of Orabella's Plan B pills or get him to buy me some.

"I forgot that you're old and would want kids by now," I teased with a smile.

"I'm not that old. You're twenty-one," he muttered into my hair. Wrapping my arms around his muscular waist, I placed my head against his chest and immediately could feel my heart swooning. Everything was perfect in his arms.

"I'll be twenty-one tomorrow," I stated. In all honesty, it

had completely erased itself from my thoughts. I never really got the chance to celebrate my birthday, so I didn't really give it much thought.

"I know, Bambolina. Why do you think we're here?" he asked. My smile seemed to grow as we just held onto each other and allowed the water to grace our skin. After a moment, we took our time lathering and massaging every inch of each other's bodies, probing my tender slit, and tantalizing his erect cock, still sensitive from stimulation.

After drying ourselves, we walked into the room, wrapped in towels, and found a bottle of champagne. There was also an assortment of cheese on a platter sitting on the table. I was quick to pop open the champagne, allowing it to fly everywhere before pouring it into a glass. I held it out for him, but he shook his head as if to say he didn't want any.

I drank the entire glass of champagne with a disgusted look on my face. It tasted bitter. I had thought that since everyone loved it in movies it would taste great—boy, was I wrong.

"Today is the best day of my entire life. No worries." I smiled as I thought about how free I felt. "No stress. There is protection and love. I love you, and thank you for all of this."

He spun me around, making me giggle, until I landed back on the floor, where he kissed me. He didn't have to say that he loved me back because I just *knew* that he did. Based on the way he looked at me and kissed me, I knew that deep down in his heart, he loved me.

When he pulled away, he pecked my lips once more, causing me to smile as I ran and jumped on top of the beautifully decorated bed. As I jumped, the towel completely slipped from my body, leaving me to flush a crimson color, quickly placing it back on.

"No, no, no. Leave it off, Anastasia," he told me, grabbing my towel. I tried to pull it back from him, but that only ended with him winning and me falling directly on top of him.

Based on the dark look in his eyes and the way he was quick to take off his towel, I knew what we were going to do for the rest of the night.

That thought left a naughty smile on my face.

ANASTASIA

*A*fter I'm not sure how many rounds, I was laid out on top of Valentino's chest with his arm around me while his other hand played with my hair. We were both awake, but we were also just deep in our own thoughts.

My eyes trailed over to the clock beside the bed to see it was after midnight. "Happy birthday to me," I whispered. There was a sadness that dawned with my words. I couldn't help it.

"Something's wrong," he stated.

I didn't say anything, provoking his hand to stop its movements in my hair. Looking up, I glanced into the blue of his eyes and saw the patience within them.

"I've never wanted a birthday celebration," I whispered just before a smile came onto my face as memories raced into my mind. "My sister always made sure I at least did something. She'd make breakfast for me and bake a cupcake with a candle on it. Every year, she'd wake me up and make me blow out the candle before singing me *Happy Birthday*. We didn't have the money to do much, but for some reason, she made it so that it never mattered whether or not we could go out. What mattered most to us was that we became one year older in a world that was so against us. It was a pure blessing that no matter what, it would always be the two of us against all evil."

A chuckle left my lips as I thought about her. Her behavior was so strong-willed and determined. There was no one in the world who could match up to Alexandria's personality. She was truly one of a kind.

"Your sister sounds wise, *no?*" he asked. I smiled, nodding my head.

"She was intelligent and wise. Sometimes, I'd forget she was younger than me," I told him, thinking about the advice she had always given me. "I just feel as though she deserves this birthday more than I do. She could've helped make the world better, I-I'm not capable of any of that," I whispered softly as my smile was replaced with a frown. His hand wandered down to my hips, pulling me up, and bringing my face closer to his.

"You're making me better, and I'm a part of the world," he pointed out. I pecked his lips before pulling away and smiling at him. My hand came up to frame his handsome face. Sometimes, I tended to forget he was actually real. He seemed too perfect to actually want me.

"I raised Enzo to be a better man than I will ever be. You need to give yourself more credit, Bambolina. You raised her to be better than you, and that means you did a perfect job." The words he said were exactly what I needed to hear.

"Thank you," I whispered.

"Happy birthday, Anastasia. We have a big day ahead of us, go to sleep," he muttered. I let out a small sigh before nodding my head against him. When my eyes shut, I could only smile as his rich smell entered my nose. *It was the place I loved to be.*

* * *

WHEN I WOKE UP, Valentino was still sleeping soundly. So, I crept out of the bed and grabbed the towel from off the floor before wrapping it around me. There were no clothes for me to change into, which made me frown. I felt completely unprepared, and I wished that he would have told me more about this surprise date earlier.

As I walked into the restroom, I was grateful for the extra pack of toothbrushes inside of one of the cupboards. I didn't know what I would do if I couldn't brush my teeth. I grabbed the blue one and immediately began my brushing routine.

After I finished, I started on my hair, which was a tangled mess. I combed through it with my fingers and then threw it up in a messy bun. Just like that, I felt absolutely clean.

Suddenly, there was a knock on the door. I glanced over at the bed to see that Valentino was still asleep. Instead of waking him, I walked over to the door and pulled it open. Valerio wore a smile on his face as he looked at me. I noticed the clothes in his hand, causing my brows to furrow in confusion.

"Hey?" I greeted, but I couldn't help the smile on my face as I looked at him. He held the bag out for me, which I took before embracing him in a hug. Every girl who worked under his management felt like they could trust him. That's what I liked most about him. I looked at him as a brother.

"Happy birthday, Barbie. Mr. Romano told me to bring these clothes for you both. I have to go, but I'll see you when you get back." He smiled as I pulled away. I returned the smile wholeheartedly, nodding my head.

"Thank you," I called out to his retreating form. He turned around briefly to wave goodbye. I shut the door and turned around, my hand digging inside of the bag he had given me. As soon as I looked up, Valentino was there leaning against the bathroom door frame with a toothbrush in his mouth.

His eyes moved down to my towel, narrowing his eyes slightly before walking into the restroom. I didn't have time to put up with his petty attitude, so I walked into the bedroom and dumped the clothes onto the bed.

Not much time passed before hands wrapped around my waist and pulled me into a hard chest.

I watched his mouth open as if he were about to say something, but then it closed. Letting out a sigh, he released me and walked out of the room.

My brows pulled together as I contemplated if I should talk to him about that or not. Then, I ultimately decided not to. I walked back over to the bed and grabbed the blue dress Valerio had packed for me. Instantly, I felt like I belonged here, like those other couples I had seen.

When my gaze trailed over to his clothes, I bit down on my lip. Then I folded them up, taking them with me into the kitchen. He was wearing boxers that hung low on his hips. The minute I walked in, he looked over at me with a raised brow.

"Here," I muttered before handing him his clothes. He took them from me as I stood there and watched him, biting down onto my lip once more. He leaned over and kissed my cheek, going on to dress himself.

"Let's go eat. There is a lot I have planned for you today," he said. I raised my brow in response as a smile played out on my face. I couldn't wait to find out what it was going to be.

"Okay, but after we finish eating, can we go pick up some Plan B's?" I asked behind a small smile as he grabbed my hand and walked me toward the kitchen. He gave me a pointed look, his eyes seemed to turn cold.

"No," he let out. I sat down in the dining room chair,

looking over at him. I wasn't sure if he was being serious or not, but I knew that I was.

"What do you mean *'no'*?" I questioned.

He sat down right across from me, running his hand through his hair. Like always, he just decided to completely ignore me by grabbing a plate of food. I didn't even notice the table full of breakfast food the employees must've brought in until now.

"Are you *trying* to get me pregnant?" I asked.

He only smirked in response, but still pretended as if I wasn't speaking to him.

I scoffed jokingly. "You are unbelievable."

ANASTASIA

*A*fter breakfast, we left to go back to the mansion. Valentino wasn't really saying much, but I didn't mind. The silence was actually calming. It allowed me to skim through my thoughts and attempt to organize them.

When we finally arrived at the mansion, we headed to his bedroom. As soon as we were in his room, he shut the door behind us, leaving me to walk over to his bed and sit down.

Eyeing him, I noticed a long velvet box in his hands. My eyes were glued to the box with raised brows. Deep down I had a feeling that whatever was in there, it would be expensive.

"Happy birthday, my Bambolina." He smiled.

My eyes followed him as he opened the box and displayed a beautiful diamond necklace. I wasn't sure how much it cost, but it was definitely expensive.

"Oh, my god! This must've cost so much!" I exclaimed, staring at it. The diamond seemed to sparkle in the light as he removed it from the box. He bit down on his lip with a raised brow, signaling for me to turn around.

I was quick to turn, and since my hair was already in a

bun, it made it easier for him to place the jewelry onto my neck and latch it into place. I gazed down at the elegant necklace in awe. It was absolutely beautiful.

"You deserve it, baby," he told me.

My eyes blurred with tears as I quickly engulfed him in a hug. His arms were quick to go around my waist. Getting on my tippy-toes, I planted my lips against his.

"Thank you! Thank you! Thank you!" I exclaimed before kissing his lips repeatedly.

He only responded by grabbing my chin and keeping my lips against his own. As he was attempting to deepen the kiss, I pulled away with a big smile on my face. Then, I glanced down at the necklace around my neck and couldn't stop looking at it.

"This is so perfect," I whispered.

If Alex could see it, she'd probably squeal until my ears bled. She was just the kind of girl who loved flowers, chocolates, and jewelry. One gift given to her would be the best gift of her life forever. She cherished things she believed to be precious.

"You think that's perfect? Imagine our children," he stated abruptly. Giving him a pointed look, I decided to ignore him and keep looking at my first-ever diamond necklace.

"Get dressed. I had one of my men put the dress I picked out for you in my closet. There are also shoes. I'll be back in a moment," he whispered before leaning over and kissing my cheek.

"Don't take too long!" I groaned just as I stood up.

"I'm not. Get dressed," he repeated.

I wasn't sure if I could actually believe him, but he walked out of the room, leaving me in there all alone. The second he was gone, I ran to the restroom, where I looked at the diamond necklace. My finger traced it as a smile graced my face. I just wish Alex could see it.

I walked out of his room and toward the closet, where I looked at the beautiful red mermaid dress. It was off-the-shoulder and seemed to be of very tight material.

Walking into the restroom, I took my hair out of the bun. It wasn't a great sight at all, so I searched everywhere for a straightener. Coming to the realization that it wasn't my bathroom, I hurriedly walked out of his bedroom and into my room, where I grabbed the iron before taking it back to Valentino's room.

It probably would've been more logical to just stay in my room, but getting ready in Valentino's space felt more official. A smile made its way onto my face as I thought back to our previous conversation.

Plugging up the flat-iron, I let it heat up before running it through my hair.

* * *

I WAS COMPLETELY DRESSED except that my dress wasn't zipped up yet. My makeup was light and presentable. I looked classy, yet very sexy.

Just as I finished, Valentino walked in. The moment his eyes moved up my entire body, I couldn't help but smile. There was a darkness in his eyes as he took me in. Turning around, I held my hair up as an indication that I needed him to zip up my dress.

He walked up to me and slowly zipped up the fabric before turning me around and planting a kiss on my cheek. "You look beautiful."

"You look even better," I whispered as my eyes drank in his appearance. He looked absolutely mouthwatering. Actually, no matter what he managed to do—he never disappointed as far as looks went.

"I doubt it," he said, his lips skimming across my ear.

Grabbing his suit, I pulled his lips toward me. His hand crept down to cup my ass as I pressed myself closer.

"We have to stop. We have reservations," he groaned against my lips before kissing down my neck.

"Fuck reservations. I want you right now, Valentino," I whispered into his ear. His hand moved up from my bottom to grip my boob in his tight hold. A moan came out of me as he caressed it in such a soothing manner.

"After," he uttered. I loved how he was telling me to stop but never managed to conclude his manipulation on me. Grabbing his hair, I moved my lips against his before allowing my tongue to enter his mouth.

"Now," I told him. Suddenly, he smacked my ass hard. I flinched and pulled away from the kiss.

"Later." He smirked. I let out an irritated groan and he chuckled lightly. He pressed the pad of his thumb against my red lips before lightly moving across them. He had red lipstick all over his lips, and I chuckled before attempting to wipe it away.

"Fine, let's go," I muttered, turning around and walking toward the door. His hand was on my lower back as he guided me through the house and out of the door. A smile graced my features at the sight of the huge black BMW parked in front of us. There was a driver inside who I had never met, but I was ready to.

* * *

THE CAR RIDE was boring only because Valentino had to yell in Italian the whole time. He was talking on the phone, 'handling business.' I knew he felt bad because he kept glancing over at me and pecking my cheek before returning to his phone.

As soon as we arrived, a man quickly sat us in the back,

where there was a private section of the restaurant all to ourselves. Everything always felt so secluded, and I actually kind of enjoyed that aspect.

"If it's important, we could always go home and you can find another way to make it up to me," I suggested, causing him to smile.

"No, you're more important," he stated.

"I'm not used to you being so nice to me. Actually, I'm not used to you being nice at all. You act like such a jerk, but I know you. I know you enough to see that you are *way* more than what you let on. You may have your organization fooled, your brother fooled, but not me," I told him truthfully before leaning back in the chair, watching him.

"You don't know me well enough then," he said so quietly that I almost didn't hear him.

"What are you talking about?" I asked.

"I am trusting you with information and I expect you to keep it, do you understand?" he asked with an arched brow.

I nodded my head slowly, as my heartbeat increased.

"Words, Anastasia. I need words," he said.

I quickly parted my lips, ready to speak. "Yes, I understand."

He sighed. "I am after Orabella's father, Dmitri Ivanov. Orabella believes her father is a good guy who died in a car accident, but it's false. Her father is responsible for the death of my family, which is why there is no mercy in my heart to say that we are only using her to get to her father."

"Please don't tell me you're planning to harm Orabella in any way. She's a young girl and no one deserves to die because they were brought into the world by the wrong parents," I pleaded.

"I would do anything to hurt Dmitri, but I don't want to hurt my brother in the process. So, no, I don't *think* I would hurt her," he responded. Despite his words, there was a look of determination and evil that loomed in his eyes. It was beginning to scare me.

"Valentino, I will love you no matter what happens. Just don't hurt that girl, please," I begged. He let out a sigh just as the waitress came. She placed our food on the table, giving a small bow as she left.

"Let's talk about this later. I don't want to ruin your day."

ANASTASIA

*W*e spent the rest of the dinner talking about everything. It felt nice to discuss things in a civil conversation. What I loved most was how much we had in common. We both suffered a great deal of hurt but continued to be strong. We were fierce warriors, and even if he didn't see it—I did.

On the drive home, he brought up my mother and asked how she was doing. Sadly, I hadn't spoken to the facility in a couple of days. They wanted to limit her visits, but a small part of me felt like I was neglecting her.

How foolish was that? She neglected me my whole life and here I am growing sad on my 'happy' day just because I feel like *I'm* neglecting *her*. With a sigh, I glanced over at Valentino, who had just finished showering. I took a shower before him, even though I would've been happier if he had joined me.

"What's wrong?" he asked. I laid back in his bed and shook my head back and forth. I wasn't going to allow my thoughts to ruin my night. It was my day, I believe I had worked so hard that I deserved it.

"Nothing," I answered.

"You started acting like this after I mentioned your mother," he mentioned. Looking off to the side, I could only shrug my shoulders. I didn't know if I was being selfish or if I was acting reasonably.

"Bambolina," he called out. I turned to look at him before sighing at the look on his face. He walked closer until he placed his fists on either side of my head, and peered down on me as he held his weight.

"I'm overthinking again. I don't know if it makes me an idiot to say that I miss my mum," I whisper as he gazes into my eyes.

"An idiot? Impossible," he said. I smiled at his words, wrapping my arms around his neck and bringing him in for a kiss. For the first time ever, it was slow and passionate. There was nothing aggressive about the kiss we shared, everything about it was perfect.

"I know a way that'll make you stop thinking so much," he whispered, pulling away slightly.

"Oh, yeah?" I challenged. "Show me."

He pulled off the shirt I was wearing, discarding it on the floor. As soon as the shirt was gone, our lips returned to their original embrace. His hand wandered down to my panties, pushing them away.

I felt him kiss down my jaw, where he displayed his affection on my skin, wandering down to my neck. His tongue moved against my skin as he sucked it. My hands roamed up to knot my fingers in Valentino's hair as my body arched all on its own as his kisses traveled even lower.

When he got to my bare breasts, his tongue swept my nipple into his mouth. He then flicked his tongue against my bud, which led to a tingling sensation deep within my center. My other breast was being kneaded by his hand.

He knelt between my legs. Starting at my knee, he kissed

up my thigh. When he reached my core, he gently licked my opening, tasting my hot, sweet wetness. Then, Valentino moved back down to my other knee and started kissing again. I moaned with desire when he reached my pussy again. He slipped a finger deep inside of me and I arched my back with pleasure.

Holding my lips open with his fingers, he dove in, fucking my hole with his tongue. I moaned and purred from the incredible pleasure. He licked up my slit until he found my clit. He slid two fingers deep inside me as he licked and sucked at my clit. My orgasm was fast approaching when he abruptly stopped all contact with any part of my cunt. I moaned pitifully and thrust my hips up and out, hoping to rub against him. He grabbed my hips to hold me still on the bed and I tried to get him to release me. Eventually, I calmed down slightly and he was able to release my hips.

I pouted on the bed until I felt something hard press against my opening. I reached down and grabbed his enormous, throbbing cock and slid it up and down my slit, lubricating him and giving myself pleasure at the same time. He soon took over and guided his cock back to my hole. I spread my legs and he gently pressed forward, allowing just his head to pop into my snatch. I moaned with pleasure as I felt him begin to stretch my hot cunt. I spread my legs wider, encouraging him to push deeper into me. However, he stood still with just his head in my pussy. I moaned, begging him to fuck me, but he still stayed in place until I was almost crying with desire. He finally pressed a little deeper, releasing a low moan from me. I arched my back, and his cock slid a little deeper into me.

Valentino then pulled all the way out, and I opened my eyes and stared straight into his eyes. He could see the pain, the desire in my eyes, and guided his cock back into me. He pressed deeper and deeper until he was completely buried in my cunt. I moaned softly and savored the feeling of being filled by his amazing cock. He began to pull out again and I was so afraid that he would pull all the way out. I quickly wrapped my legs around him, forcing him back inside of me. He laughed softly, seeing my desperation, and finally gave in.

He started out slow, with long, deliberate strokes in and out of my dripping core. He quickly developed a rhythm that kept me moaning with pleasure. Soon, I was crying out as I felt my orgasm coming fast. I kept my legs wrapped around him, afraid that he might try to deprive me of another orgasm. Luckily, he wasn't that cruel, as his mouth came into contact with my own. He was thrusting in and out of me at a slow pace. For some reason, it made everything more intense.

I cried out against his lips as I climaxed, and he began to go harder and faster. As I came down from my sexual high, he broke the kiss to move over to my neck as he began to pummel in and out of me at a faster pace. I was moaning and breathing heavily as I could feel myself growing even wetter around his cock.

He then licked my nipple before sucking the entire thing into his mouth. My eyes rolled back at the feel of him sucking against my skin as his cock slid in and out of me.

"Don't stop," I moaned. His mouth then moved over to my other nipple where he continued the manipulations. My body felt on fire even while he thrust in and out of me at his now leisurely place. It felt as though he was prolonging our moment together. The time played no factor in our love-making as he coaxed my insides. He was massaging my walls as I squeezed around him, never wanting it to end.

When his fingers went up to my mouth, I quickly flicked my tongue against them before sucking. His eyes grew dark as they shut momentarily before his pumping inside of me increased once again.

My body tensed as I came around him for the second time. My clit was sensitive and tired, leaving me to let out a small moan as he came. Shortly after, he began to grow limp inside of me, allowing me to catch my breath. I realized that it was the second time he had come inside of me, and being as kind as I was, I just decided not to comment on it.

He slid out of me with ease just before grabbing onto my neck and kissing me once again. I pulled away softly with a smile on my face while he grabbed the blanket and spread it out on top of us. I felt his arm around my waist before he lowered himself down and pressed his lips against my belly.

"Okay, I wasn't going to say anything when you decided to come inside of me, but you're *really* pushing it now," I muttered, pinching his neck. He didn't even care. To prove that my pinching had no effect on him, he decided to kiss my belly once more.

"You're so annoying." I smiled.

"I'm annoying because I want my girlfriend to have my children?" he asked, chuckling against my skin. Rolling my eyes, I moved to pinch him again, but he was quick to grab my hand.

"Girlfriend?" I laughed; his hand pulled me closer to him as I let out a sigh of contentment.

"*I don't want you to ever leave me,*" he said seriously. I raised a brow as I looked down into his eyes. There was a sadness that shined so bright, it left a frown on my face.

"What did you say?" I asked, growing extremely curious. I knew his words were heavy based on the way his eyes held mine.

"I'm going to be out for a couple of days trying to locate Dmitri's place. It won't be long," he stated. I watched him move away from my stomach and over to the other side of the bed. He switched off the lamp and then returned to lay right beside me

"Fine. Thank you again for today," I whispered. He pecked my lips before pulling back. My arms were quick to wrap around him in an embrace. For the first time, he actually let me hold him in a way that resembled a hug. It felt nice.

"Don't expect this treatment tomorrow," he stated. I pulled away from him with an eye-roll. Turning over, I didn't even want to look at him after that statement. He always managed to ruin every moment with his asshole behavior.

His hand was quick to grip my hip, wrapping around my waist and pulling me back into his chest. I didn't care to look at him, my gaze wandered over to the window as the moonlight danced around the room.

"I was kidding, Bambolina." He chuckled before planting a kiss on the back of my neck. His hand started to rub my stomach soothingly until I realized what he was doing. He was rubbing my belly as if it were swollen and round with a baby inside of my womb.

"Valentino, *stop*," I groaned. He only laughed softly in response, continuing exactly what he was doing. Sometimes, I questioned why my heart seemed to care so much for this man. Maybe it saw what many eyes couldn't—a broken boy scared to show how broken he truly was.

"What if I don't?" he asked huskily. A smirk made its way onto my face as I turned to face him. My gaze fell to his lips before I brought my finger up to trace them. They were so plump and pink, everything about them was incredibly kissable.

"I'll pinch you," I answered, giggling like a schoolgirl.

"Oh, yeah?" he asked. Nodding my head with a look of confidence wasn't a good idea. Instead of rubbing my stomach, he ended up using his fingers to tickle me. My laugh boomed, leaving me short of breath.

"Stop!" I exclaimed, trying to pull his hand away from my

belly. No matter how hard I tried, his tickling never ended. My stomach was beginning to hurt from laughing so much.

"Val—I'm sorry—stop!" I called out. Finally, he stopped tickling me, and I sobered up with a few giggles.

"I had no clue you were so ticklish." He laughed. I pushed his shoulder, leaving him to only laugh harder. The smile on my face never eased as I stared at him. He had a beautiful laugh. It was deep and rich—it was also a sound so rare that it left butterflies fluttering in my stomach.

"Don't talk to me for the rest of the night," I muttered with a smile still on my face. Actually, I didn't want him to stop talking to me. I just wanted an excuse to get him to continue acting like he was more than just some mob boss. He was a man with feelings, and he was trusting me enough to be vulnerable.

"You don't mean that," he told me, burying his face into the crook of my neck from behind.

"You're still talking to me," I huffed, pretending to sound irritated. His hand ran down to my stomach, but just before he could actually tickle me, I managed to pinch him.

"Stop," he told me, lifting his head up from my neck.

"*You* stop," I responded. Our eyes met, both of us smiling like idiots. We were acting like kids, but it was perfectly okay. We were barely given the chance to be kids when it was time for us to be. I watched his smile slowly disappear. His eyes shed off a seriousness that caused me to furrow my brows.

"I love you," he said.

I could feel my heart literally stop. I was so sensitive I felt the need to instantly cry. My smile grew even more as I turned completely around to gaze at him. He actually said that he—*Valentino Romano*—loves me.

"I love you," I whispered before pecking his cheek. I pulled back and allowed my hand to caress his cheek before meeting his lips once more. "Thank you."

"Why are you thanking me?" he asked. Suddenly, I felt myself grow even more emotional. I didn't mean to say thank you, but it just slipped out.

"Thank you for loving me. I haven't heard those words in—I don't know how long, but I'm so happy to hear that I'm actually loved by someone again," I told him, biting down on my lip.

"I should be thanking you for loving me despite my flaws. You're an amazing woman, Anastasia. I'm sorry for not realizing that sooner," he stated. My arms were quick to wrap around his neck as he held my waist.

Everything felt perfect, but all good things must always come to an end.

ANASTASIA

$\mathcal{V}$alentino wasn't wrong about him having to leave for a couple of days. With him being gone, I guess that also meant Vincenzo had to be with him. The mansion was empty with just me and Orabella. We had gotten closer over the past few days, and I really enjoyed calling her my friend.

I made my way to Orabella's room to find that she had just woken up.

"You're here! I wanted to ask you something," Orabella said. "My clothes have been getting a little too small, and I desperately need new things. Do you think we could maybe go to the mall?"

I bit down on my lip as I thought about it. Even though the men were away, I knew that they still caught wind of everything.

"Okay, I'll ask Valerio to make sure it's okay," I told her. She let out a huff of annoyance but didn't say anything else as I walked out of the room and down the hallway toward the club. The security guy was there with a cold look on his face.

"I need to talk to Valerio," I muttered before crossing my arms over my chest.

The security man gave a curt nod before speaking Italian into the microphone by his lips.

Not long after, Valerio strolled into the mansion with a smile on his face. "What can I do for you, Barbie?"

"Orabella needs to go to the mall. Do you think you could maybe run that by Valentino?" I questioned.

"Of course. I was scheduled to talk to him in a few minutes…" Just as he said that his phone began to ring. He flashed me a smile before answering and pressing it to his ear.

"Sir. Before we begin, Anastasia wanted to ask you if it was okay for her and Orabella to go to the mall," he asked.

I hated asking for permission, but I wasn't a complete idiot. Going to the mall could be unsafe. I was sure that being in the Mafia must've meant there were a lot of enemies. I wasn't going to risk my life for a few clothes, at least not without safety precautions.

"He wants to speak with you," Valerio said before handing his phone over to me.

I grabbed it from his hand and pressed it against my ear.

"Bambolina," he said into the phone.

I turned around to face away from Valerio, seeing as his voice made me blush. It sounded sexier over the phone.

"Valentino." I smiled. "Is everything okay?"

"Of course, baby," he said. My cheeks grew a deeper color of pink. It was crazy how much of an effect he had on me.

"Enzo and I will be home in an hour. Valerio said you wanted to go to the mall, *no?*" he questioned.

I nodded before the realization of him not seeing me crossed my mind. Turning around to glance at Valerio, I saw that he was talking to the guard in Italian. My attention turned back to the phone as he awaited my reply.

"Yes, Orabella wants to go. Will you be joining us?" I asked, my voice trying to keep its desperation inside.

It wasn't helping much, seeing as hope still lingered in my words.

"I still have a few things to take care of. Valerio will accompany you both to make sure nothing happens," he said. "I have to talk to Valerio, but I'll see you when I get home, Bambolina."

"Okay," I said, even though I didn't want to give the phone back. I just wanted to stay there forever.

"I love you," he told me. My smile grew tenfold. Once again, I glanced over at Valerio to see he was still busy.

"I love you more." I smiled. Before he could say anything, I handed the phone back to Valerio and ran up the stairs to tell Orabella the news. When I walked into her room, she was still lying down on her bed with the blanket over her head.

"Hey, you okay?" I asked. Suddenly, a feeling of déjà vu rushed into my system as I looked at her. *No, she's not Alex.*

"I have a headache," she groaned.

I sat down on her bed and pressed my hand against her forehead to check if she was sick. When I didn't feel any excessive temperature change, I smiled gently.

"Valentino said we can go to the mall," I told her.

She quickly shot up before jumping out of her bed. Chuckling softly, I stood up and walked over to the bathroom door.

"Are you still up for it?" I questioned.

Based on how happy she looked, I was sure that I'd already received my answer. "Yes! It's nothing that some medicine can't fix!" she cheered.

Rolling my eyes playfully, I began to walk toward her door before turning around.

"I think the brothers will be home in about an hour. So, get dressed. I'll be back," I told her.

"Okay!" she shouted happily.

Smiling, I opened the door and strolled down the stairs. I headed all the way to the other side of the mansion to my bedroom. It was quite difficult to walk from Orabella's room to mine, seeing as they were located on opposite sides of the house.

When I finally made it to my room, I walked into my closet. Most of my clothing was pink. The person who bought my clothes must've *really* thought I was a Barbie doll. With a sigh, I grabbed a pink top and a pair of blue jeans before slipping on a pair of cute sandals.

After doing my hair and getting dressed, I made my way to Orabella's room. Just as I walked in, she was putting on her jeans and a tube top. She smiled at me through the full-length mirror in her closet as I stepped further into the room.

"I haven't seen much of Vincenzo," Orabella told me as she applied some lip gloss.

Her hair was fluffed out in thick, dark waves, which looked really pretty on her. Then, she puckered her lips in the mirror before turning to face me.

"I haven't seen much of Valentino either," I told her honestly.

I wasn't sure what I was supposed to tell her. I also wasn't sure if it was my place to. A frown took over my face as I thought about all of the information I had to keep from her.

"You ready?" she asked me. Her eyes trailed down to look at my outfit. I smiled at the look of acceptance she shared.

"You clean up nicely." She winked.

"Why, thank you. You don't look too bad yourself," I returned, just as flirty, before walking out of the room with Orabella by my side.

We both strolled down the stairs and walked out of the door. Valerio was already waiting for us with the back door open. As we both climbed in, the door closed behind us. Quickly, after the guard had gotten inside and started up the car—we were on our way.

As soon as we were off down the road, I looked over at Orabella with a smirk on my face. "How are things between you and Mr. Rossi?"

"Really good. Call me crazy, but I don't think I've ever met a man like him before," she told me truthfully.

I bit down on my lip to keep from showing my guilt.

"What about you and Mr. Valentino Romano?" she questioned.

"If only you knew." I laughed.

Orabella was smiling at me as we finally pulled into the mall's parking lot. As soon as she opened the door, her stomach contents spilled out of her mouth and onto the parking lot floor.

I quickly leaned over and grabbed ahold of her hair, holding it in place so it didn't get in her vomit. When she finished, she spit onto the ground, attempting to get the taste out of her mouth.

"Here," Valerio said.

Orabella gazed up to see the water bottle he had in his hand. Taking it from him, she unscrewed the cap and poured the water into her mouth before spitting it out on the ground.

"Talk about great timing," I sighed, letting go of her hair and leaning back in the seat. It would've been terrible if she threw up in the car.

"Are you sick? Do you want to return home?" Valerio asked kindly. Shaking her head, Orabella took another swig of water.

"My stomach probably didn't like that crawfish I ate earlier." She laughed before patting her stomach.

He nodded before opening my door and letting us both out.

"You sure you're all right? We can go to the mall tomorrow," I said, raising my hand up to check her forehead again. Alex had a fever the entire time she had cancer and I never noticed. Even when she complained of aches all the time—I never noticed. Maybe if I had detected signs sooner, I could've saved her.

"I promise, I'm okay. Sometimes seafood and I don't really get along," she told me as she reached down to grasp my hand. I was dragged by Orabella to the front door of the mall. I let out a sigh and decided to calm down.

The moment we walked in, Orabella smiled. When she looked over at me, I had the exact same smile. We were both thinking the exact same thing—we're about to go ballistic.

* * *

AFTER HOURS OF SHOPPING, we were finally home. Orabella looked like she was scared about something, leaving me to worry for her. Every time I asked her about it, she would shake her head and look elsewhere. It made me concerned, but I didn't want to say much about it.

When we arrived home, Orabella was slow to grab all of her bags, so I took that time to go inside. Valentino was walking toward the door. The second I saw him, I pulled him into a hug before pecking his lips.

Just as I was about to ask him about his day, Orabella walked in. She didn't even bother to look at me as she walked straight up to Valentino. He *hated* her. I could see it in his eyes as he looked at the girl. Frowning at them, I stayed silent and resorted to observing. I just hoped he would soon realize that whatever happened to him and his brother wasn't her fault.

"Where's Vincenzo?" she asked him. His eyes continued to look at me even though he was talking to her.

"Here's an idea, princess," he said, finally averting his dangerously cool eyes from me. He looked over at Orabella, taking a step toward her. "How about you look like a big girl?"

Rolling her eyes, she carried on up the stairs.

"Really, Valentino?" I pronounced the moment she wasn't in hearing range.

He rolled his eyes and walked down the hall toward his room. I followed right behind him, already growing irritated by his actions.

When we made it to his room, I overlooked the anger in his face. His clenched fists and jaw were enough to make me frown.

"I don't want to talk about this. I need you," he stated. He pulled me into his chest and started to kiss my neck.

"Okay, but I just want you to know that hate and revenge won't fix anything. The pain will always be there. Take it from me," I said, hoping to get him to understand where I was coming from.

He let out a sigh before he pulled away. Based on the hard look in his eye, he didn't care. He didn't even *want* to care. His heart was set on revenge and that was all.

"I'm gonna go shower," he grumbled. I could only watch as he walked away.

ANASTASIA

*M*any days had passed, and Valentino allowed me to strip again. I think it was his way of distracting me from what he was planning. I didn't mind the distraction. I was happy that it meant I didn't have to face Orabella much. There was no way I could look her in the eye while lying to her. She didn't deserve what Valentino was trying to do.

As I walked through the club, my eyes met Valentino's. He was looking at me with an expression thatI couldn't quite decipher. I was quick to glance away and walk toward the back. We hadn't really spoken much the past few days because he would only get busier. I missed him, but I didn't want to get in the way of his work.

My shift was almost over, and as soon as it finished, I'd be joining Sarah in the kitchen to eat, because I was starving.

When I turned back to where Valentino was, he was gone. A huge part of me actually wanted him to come talk to me.

After exiting the club, I made my way to the kitchen to see if there was anything I could eat. My stomach was killing me.

"Hey, Sarah," I called out. She turned to face me with a bright smile on her face.

I laid my head down on the counter as I bent over and folded my arms over my head. My entire lower region was hurting.

"You okay?" she asked.

I stood up and nodded my head. "Yes, if it's okay, I was wondering if you could cook me something, because I'm starving."

She quickly nodded her head and began to gather things to cook. "Of course! I have already begun to cook a little something."

It was only then that I was welcomed by the beautiful aroma of freshly cooked foods.

Sadly, my happiness for the food didn't last long because a pissed-off Vincenzo walked down the stairs and straight toward me. His facial expression scared me to the core. I didn't understand what I had done, so I stayed frozen in my spot.

"You," Vincenzo called out. "Come here."

I walked toward him, feeling as if I were walking on shaky ground.

"I'm going to ask you a question. Then, I'm going to need you to think long and hard about the answer. If you try to *lie* to me, I will have no problem showing you what happens to a liar," he threatened. "Where the hell is Orabella?"

My body completely froze. I honestly didn't know all the details about the plan. I had no clue where she was, or how exactly Valentino planned to hurt her father. All I knew was that he was taking a huge risk.

"I swear I don't know," I told him, my voice breaking in fear. Raising a brow, he folded his arms across his chest before nodding his head slowly.

"You don't know, huh?" he quizzed. I looked up at him

pleadingly, just hoping he understood that I was telling the truth.

Recognition coaxed his face as he hurriedly walked out of the house. A frown took over my features as I quickly grabbed my phone from in my pocket. When I tried to call Valentino, I couldn't help but worry when it went straight to voicemail.

"Orabella is missing?" Sarah asked, setting my plate down in front of me.

As worry filled my brain, I ate my food, hoping that everything was okay. If anything were to happen to Orabella, I didn't know how I would ever forgive him. I promised I would always be by his side no matter what, but Orabella wasn't just some pawn he could manipulate. She was a human with a heart of gold.

I tried to rack my brain for all the possible situations that Valentino probably put her in. He informed me that he wanted to use her to get to Dmitri. *What the hell could that mean?*

"I don't know," I answered Sarah.

Picking up my phone, I called his number again and again. Each time I called, it went straight to voicemail.

I ran into Valentino's room, where I began looking for something…anything. There had to be some way to know what he planned for her.

Then, my mind raced over to a folder I had seen a while ago. It was right by his nightstand the last time I had seen it. With my brows pulled together, I wandered over to the nightstand, but the folder was no longer there.

It wasn't until I opened a drawer that I finally found it. I picked up the folder and sat it down on his bed, where I could see several photos of Dmitri, and then Orabella when she was younger. There were threatening notes from Dmitri, stating he wanted to start a war. Not only that, but Dmitri went into detail about what he had done to Valentino's family. He mentioned how he began with his mother, and how funny he thought it was when he moved on to Valentino's stepfather. Dmitri even went as far as mentioning how Valentino was nothing but a boy working too hard to get back something he would never have again.

My shoulders fell as I read over the notes, all of them graphic and painful. It made sense now why Valentino was so adamant about revenge. It was hard not to when the murderer of every person you held dear only served as a reminder of them.

VALENTINO

*W*hen my brother told me about his suspicions of Orabella possibly being pregnant, I almost lost it. There was no way he wanted to take part in the plan we had been constructing our entire lives. Even when I told him that Dmitri was coming in a week with plans to bring down our entire organization to get his daughter, Vincenzo didn't care.

It didn't make sense to me how he could be so careless over that girl. I wished I actually wanted to respect my brother's request for us to drop the mission, but I couldn't. He didn't have to go through the nightmares of that day—I did. Luckily for him, he couldn't remember the way our mother's eyes stared at me as she begged for someone to help her. He wasn't able to understand that our whole family looked to me in order to save them, and I didn't. Vincenzo was so fucking lucky that he didn't have to go downstairs and clean up all the splatters of blood left in the house. He didn't have to live through that shit, but I did.

To think that he wanted to save the girl who was raised by the man who did this to me drove me insane. He could get any girl in the world pregnant to carry-on our name, but he chose that stupid whore who deserved every bit of wrath because of her father.

It was the only reason why I called her down to my office, where I explained to her that her whole life was a lie. I wanted to smile at the tears that fell from her eyes when she realized her father wasn't as innocent as she thought he was.

It was the only reason why I convinced her to come with me to pay him a visit. Hate fluttered around in her eyes at the thought of him, but she agreed. Just like I wanted her to, *she agreed* now knowing that my plans weren't just for her to go talk to him. I wanted her to kill him. That was what he deserved. He deserved to have the person he loved most in the world be the same person who struck him with a bullet. She was so entranced with the love she grew with my brother, that my bad intentions evaporated from her eyes.

She got in the car with me, and we drove off to Dmitri's place. My men had helped me track it down. I could tell she was angry.

"I just want you to know that I am sorry he did that to you. There is no one in the world who deserves what you and Vincenzo had to go through," Orabella let out. "I'll talk to him and tell him to back off about trying to get me back because I want to stay. I want to stay with Vincenzo and never speak to my father again. I promise you that."

I only glared at her in response. It didn't take long for us to arrive at Dmitri's safehouse, which remained less guarded than normal.

Orabella let out a loud sigh before looking at me. "I really am sorry, okay? I hope this proves where my loyalty lies."

"Go talk to him, and if they ask where you came from, say you escaped from Vincenzo. I'll be waiting right here," I lied. There was no way I was going to wait. As soon as she went in there, I would be joining her shortly after, to force her to partake in the death of her father.

Orabella glanced at me nervously before getting out of the car and heading straight to the door. I noticed one of the guards had opened the entrance, and he immediately recognized Orabella. Thanks to the bush that helped hide my car, when he looked around for anyone, he found nothing.

Soon, the man let her in.

I immediately called my soldier, Killian, and informed him that she was in the building, so it was time to send men in to take down all of Dmitri's guards. We couldn't handle anything going wrong.

After a few moments of waiting for Killian's response, I moved in. I entered the home with my gun in hand, prepared for anything to come at me. My gaze looked sharply for anyone, but I was glad to not detect a single figure.

"You lied to me! My entire life all you have done is lie! How could you?" I could hear Orabella's shouts coming from Dimitri's living room.

As I turned a corner to track the source of her voice, I could see her yelling at Dmitri, the man I truly despised. His short gray hair, paling skin, and wrinkles making their appearance.

It didn't take long for him to notice me. When he did, he looked over at his daughter in shock. I was glad to see how much sadness reaped from his face.

"You set me up?" he asked her.

I held my gun with a smirk on my face. It had been so long that I wanted to see him with the barrel of a gun pointed directly at him. It was karma. I remember when I had been in his same position twenty years ago—*scared and hurt.*

"She did." I laughed. "Orabella, come here, doll."

She hesitated, but with one look at the gun in my hand, she came over to where I stood.

"You told me you were going to prove to me where your loyalty lies, so do it. Prove it to me," I growled.

Her eyes widened when I handed her a different gun. It was small, but it could cause just as much damage as any gun could.

"What? No! This isn't part of the plan!" Orabella shouted. Her eyes were wide as she held the gun. Despite it being small, it looked big in her tiny hands.

Suddenly, her dad made a move at her, leaving her to aim the gun at him. Her breathing was heavy as she stared at her father. There was a quiver as she held the gun. Perspiration coated her forehead and her chest was rising and falling dramatically.

"Stay back, Dad!" she yelled out. "Is it true what he told me? Did you actually kill his family in front of him?"

"Orabella, don't do this," he pleaded.

"Answer the question!"

I smirked at the disappointment that lurked in his eyes as he looked between his daughter and me. His heart was breaking, and I knew it. *That's right, Dimitri, you are finally getting a taste of what I felt all those years ago.*

Dmitri wasn't going to make it out alive, and I wanted to make sure that it would hurt him in the worst possible way.

"It's true. Roberto and his wife were planning on destroying our alliance before a big feud and I felt like I couldn't depend on their loyalty any longer. It was stupid, but I have only wanted to protect you from this life. I know I made mistakes, and it may change your view of me, but the love I have for you has always been real," he let out desperately, completely changing the subject.

She was staring at him with a lone tear falling from her eyes. I could see that her thoughts were sprinting through her mind. I couldn't believe that the foolish girl actually listened to him. He was a manipulative liar, and it ran deep in his blood.

"I can't," she whispered. I watched as she began to lower her gun, so I decided to take it upon myself to shoot him over and over again. I wanted as many bullets to penetrate his body to equal the amount he used to murder everyone I loved.

"No!" Orabella shouted as she began to run over to her father's dead body. Just as I was about to roll my eyes, a figure appeared in the corner of my vision. The same guard who opened the door for Orabella had his gun cocked and ready for her.

Orabella was so worried about her father that she didn't see the bullet piercing through the air. As quickly as I could, I took off in the direction of her body, hoping to block the bullet from penetrating her. By the time I reached her, it was already too late.

She fell to the ground with a gasp. Before checking to see if she was okay, I immediately aimed my gun in his direction shot him right between the eyes. When I was sure he was dead, I dropped down to falling to the girl, trying my best to aid her.

She had been shot in her chest, but there was no exit wound, meaning the bullet was still lodged in her body.

"Fuck! Hey, stay with me, okay?" I asked her, my chest rising n falling. She groaned as her face grimaced in pain. I reached for the phone inside my pocket before calling a doctor friend of mine who agreed to rush her to the hospital.

"Tell…Vince…I'm…so…sorry," she cried. Fuck! Vincenzo was going to hate me. I knew he had feelings for this girl, but I let greed get in the way. Just like that, I may have just lost my brother. The realization ate away at my cold heart.

"Keep talking. Tell me about Vincenzo," I urged her, praying that she wouldn't die.

Her eyes were starting to blink more slowly until she stopped blinking at all. I made sure to press down on her chest to control the bleeding, but blood still oozed out of her.

"He is so pretty. He is so kind and smart. I think I love him, and even though he took me from my home, I was grateful to be free of that *hell*. He was my savior, and I am so glad to have met...him," she muttered, her voice growing weaker with each word. Her every word made my heart drop even more. She said she loves him. The dying girl in my arms loved my little brother, and I was sure he loved her too.

"Keep talking. Come on, Orabella, don't stop," I said desperately. When she didn't respond I shook her body, trying to get any word from her mouth only for her head to lifelessly roll to the side.

"Fuck!"

ANASTASIA

Sarah had gratefully gotten the location where Orabella and Valentino were. My heart dropped when she told me they were at the hospital. I prayed they were both okay.

I hurriedly made my way to the hospital, the place I'd really begun to hate with every fiber in my body. The moment I arrived, I could see Orabella being pushed through the halls. My jaw dropped when I noticed she was covered in blood. Nurses and doctors were rushing her into a room, and I tried to follow but was pushed back.

"Orabella!" I shouted, tears falling from my eyes.

I tried to find Valentino, but he was nowhere to be found. Worry clouded my mind as I hoped he wasn't hurt.

I picked up my phone and tried dialing Valentino's number again, but it wouldn't go through. It kept going straight to voicemail. This undying need to scream settled within me. I couldn't handle the thought of losing someone I loved again.

"I'm sorry, ma'am, but you're going to have to go back to the waiting room," one of the nurses said. A sharp, shooting pain erupted in my lower region. I looked down to see blood trailing down my legs as black dots began to cloud my vision.

"Oh, my God!" the nurse shouted just before everything went black.

* * *

I WOKE up to the sound of my heart monitor beeping repeatedly. My eyes almost shot out of my head as I looked around to notice I was in a hospital room. A doctor walked into the room, wearing a kind smile.

"Hi, how are you feeling?" the doctor questioned.

"What happened?" I asked as the pounding in my head reminded me of the blood I had seen running down my leg.

"You passed out, and after I learned you were here for Orabella Martinez, I have reason to believe your stress played a huge factor. We did a pelvic exam, and I'm so sorry," her voice cracked as she looked at me. "You had a miscarriage."

"I had a baby?" I asked, my eyes shut as I laid on top of the table.

My eyes moved up to look at the light above my head. My body was shaking, and I knew it was because I was crying. There were no sounds to be heard. All I could hear was my slowing heartbeat as I thought about my baby.

"I am so sorry." She frowned. "There is nothing wrong with your body. I checked and ran a few tests. As I mentioned, my only assumption is that the stress of your friend really took its toll on you."

I didn't bother to say another word as my eyes stared at the wall in front of me.

"When can I leave?" I cried.

"I'll go get your discharge papers," the doctor muttered sadly before walking out of the room.

"Yellow, like the sun after rain," Alex told me. *"The way it beams on every piece of land—you love every part of everyone just the same."*

I couldn't stop my tears as the memory played out in my mind. I knew she only existed in my imagination, but I needed her. I needed my little sister back. Everything was always better when she was with me.

"Every person you touch, you make them better," she whispered before running her hand through my hair. *"That's why I admire you, Anastasia. You are so beautiful on the inside, just like the color yellow."*

I knew now that she was nothing but a liar. If that were true, why was I lying in a hospital bed all alone? Every person I touched, I damaged. Just like Orabella, just like my sister, and now, just like my baby.

The doctor came back with my discharge papers. I didn't have any extra clothes, but the doctor gave me some that they kept for patients. Weakly, I threw on the clothes. She tried to tell me about therapists I could talk to and support systems I should have, but I was too far gone for that kind of thing.

I exited the hospital room and traveled down the halls until I could find Orabella in the small hospital. Before I went home to cry my eyes out, I at least wanted to make sure that Orabella was okay.

After a long walk, I finally caught sight of the raven-haired girl. My lips parted in shock as I looked at her. So many tubes and wires were attached to her body, leaving me to pull my brows together.

Just as I was about to take a step closer to her, the sound of Valentino's voice hit me. A feeling of relief flooded through my body as I found myself turning to see him. However, when Vincenzo pushed by with a deep scowl on his face, I knew things weren't good.

"This is why I can't wait to get the hell away from you!" Vincenzo seethed. "Look at what the fuck you did! I told you to let this stupid plan of yours go. If Orabella had died, I would have *killed* you! I mean it!"

I gasped at his words as my frown slumped deeper at the sight of hurt flashing in Valentino's eyes. He didn't say another word to his brother before walking off. Then, he paused when he saw me.

"Val—"

"Just shut the hell up! I know, already. I know I'm a monster, and I don't give a fuck about it. Just like I don't give a fuck about you or your opinions!" he growled.

Without another word, he walked away from me.

I ran past the room, down the hall, and out to the parking lot. I needed to take a shower and wipe all of the blood off of me before Valentino could see it. I didn't want to make him sad or feel the loss of the child he had always wanted. It was completely my fault. I lost our baby. There was no way I could face his disappointment.

He walked right past me as if I meant nothing.

As I leaned against my car, I broke down. Sobs were bubbling out of me, and my tears were falling nonstop. Suddenly, a hand gripped my shoulder, shocking me to turn around. Seeing that it was Vincenzo, surprise stirred in me

"Are you okay?" he asked. I hiccupped as I nodded with a small smile. My tears still wouldn't stop falling.

"Orabella is going to be fine. They have her sedated to make things less painful for her, but they said she will be awake by tomorrow," he informed me. I was glad she would be okay, it felt nice to finally receive some good news. "I feel bad for the way I spoke to my brother. He may not be the best person in the world, but he's done a lot for me and so little for himself. Even if he almost killed my girlfriend, I know he's beating himself up for it more than anyone else could. I know my brother enough to say that he didn't mean anything he just said to you. He gets like that sometimes, where he pushes people away. Don't let him do it to you."

Wiping away my tears, I nodded my head.

"Thank you," I whispered.

* * *

DECIDING to take Vincenzo's advice, I drove all the way to the mansion. Determined, I made my way to Valentino's bedroom, where I gently pushed open the door. All of the lights were off, but I was able to make him out on the bed, gazing up at the ceiling. I walked over to the mattress and crawled in until I was beside him. Before I could say or do anything, his arm wrapped around me and pulled me into his warmth.

Instantly, I broke down crying once again. I felt so lost and alone just being without him for two seconds. My head hurt from crying so much, and as his hand glided down my back, my crying only increased. His arms were around me as I wept. None of us said a word, he just allowed me to lay in his arms and let everything out.

I wish I knew how to tell him that so much happened in such a short amount of time. Nothing felt fair, someone was punishing me for something, but I just couldn't figure out what for.

"I lost the baby," I whispered as tears soaked into the pillow. His eyes met mine and he could see all of the pain I held. I was crying more than I had ever cried in my life.

"You were pregnant?" he asked.

"I didn't know I was, but I never want to be pregnant again. Everyone dies. My sister died, my baby died," I sobbed.

My head rested in the crook of his neck as he held me. I could feel my body shaking as shock surrounded my heart in an attempt to protect me with numbness. Nothing felt real anymore.

"*Shh,*" he cooed while lifting up my shirt and rubbing my bare skin up and down. I took that time to try my best to calm down. My body was still shaking and I could feel hiccups escaping me as I tried my best to stop crying. Tears never brought anyone or anything back.

"I...I..." I tried to speak, but my words wouldn't even form.

"Breathe," he said softly to me.

I listened to his words and slowed my breathing as much as I could. Making sure I focused on a deep breath in and a deep breath out, the world seemed to ease around me. I was feeling as though I was suffocating, but slowly everything seemed to calm.

"What's wrong with me?" I asked, my voice finally relaxed.

My sadness didn't allow my voice to sound like it normally did. It left me sounding like a disappointed child trying their best to no longer be broken.

"It's my fault. I'm sorry for everything. You were right," he explained.

My breathing was beginning to pick up, and his hand on my back ran up to my hair as he soothed me by simply caressing me.

"I know you didn't mean to hurt her, and I know that Orabella's father had hurt you. I told you I would be there for you no matter what," I whispered.

The feeling of wanting to cry again was quick to wash through my emotions.

At first, a baby had never crossed my mind, now it was all I could think about. My heart broke a little more as I thought about my entire family—Mum, Alex, the baby, and I—all just at the park and running around the swing-set.

My life was supposed to be easy. I expected to claim my happily ever after. The truth was that in reality, there was no such thing as being happy forever.

A tear escaped before I had a chance to stop it.

"I know you really wanted a baby, and I'm so sorry that I couldn't have it. There is no happy with me, Valentino. You deserve someone who is happy," I whispered, my voice still breaking in sadness.

"There's no one in the world I could ever imagine having children with other than you," he told me.

I wanted to cry at the possibility of that never happening. Silence settled around us as he hugged me tightly.

"I need to, um, shower," I whispered before getting up on shaky feet.

My balance was so off that I almost fell, but Valentino was quick to get up and let me lean on him for support.

Before I could apologize, he swept me off my feet and held me like a newlywed bride. He walked me into the bathroom before sitting me down on the counter. I could only watch him with a numbness coating my heart as he turned on the shower.

He walked up to me with his hands on my hips before pecking my cheek. I couldn't even allow myself to have an expression. Everything still felt so wrong. Being happy felt wrong. He lifted my shirt off of me before taking off the shorts that the hospital had given. The fresh panties I got from the hospital were already covered in blood, and as I looked down, I sucked in a breath and started crying once more.

He was going to realize that I'm incapable of doing something like carrying his baby. I was a disgrace, which is exactly why Alex should be alive instead of me.

"Shh, it's okay," he whispered before bringing me into his chest.

I knew what he was doing—he was trying not to allow me to see it, but it was stuck on repeat in my brain. *It was my baby.*

He peeled off my panties, which only resulted in me crying more as I wrapped my arms around his neck and sobbed into the crook of his neck. He pulled them down until they were off my legs before allowing his hand to climb up to the clasp of my bra. He undid the clasp and then took it off of me.

When I turned slightly to look in the mirror, I could see how much of a mess I looked. My makeup was a wreck and my hair was so tangled. Not to mention the fact that my blue eyes were left dull and lifeless.

Turning my attention back to Valentino, he had finished removing his shirt along with his pants before he pushed down his boxers. When he finished, he grabbed a hold of my hand and helped me down from the counter before walking me into the huge shower.

I wrapped my hands around his waist as I continued to lay against his chest. My eyes shut as he grabbed some soap and began to wash my entire body. The silence that settled around us was calming.

My mind was empty, my heart was empty, everything just felt *empty. How does a person get over killing the life of one who never got the chance to even live?*

"Anastasia, look at me," he said.

He kissed the top of my head as I craned my neck up to look at him. I could see the broken look in his eyes as well. I never took into account how hurt he must've felt. He was the one who really wanted a baby.

"You did nothing wrong. Some things happen, and I know you're hurt, but maybe it wasn't the best time to have a child. Your body knew it, and one day when things are better, we'll try for another one. I love you, baby, don't forget that I'm here," he said softly. I nodded as I brought my face into his neck once more.

"I love you," I cried. His arms tightened around me. I felt safe and I felt home. "We would've made amazing parents. I took care of Alex; you took care of Vince—I can't stop thinking about how different our child's life would be compared to the lives we were given. We've been hurt so much, why are we still hurting?"

He was starting to wash my hair, and he wasn't saying a word. When I looked up, there was a tear falling from his eye, or maybe it was the shower.

"You? You don't deserve all of the terrible things that keep happening to you. Me? I deserve it all. I'm a bad man, Anastasia," he explained.

Shaking my head, I pulled away from his neck to look into his eyes.

"You're not a bad man. I know you feel bad for what happened to Orabella. When you looked me in the eye and told me you wouldn't hurt her, I didn't see a lie. She's strong, and I know she will be okay. You are not the devil, you're just a hurt man. If you look too closely, you can't see that the devil and a hurt man are so similar that they can appear to be the same," I told him. His eyes gazed into mine before he leaned down to peck my lips. When he pulled away, he kissed my cheek before kissing the top of my head.

After the shower, he turned off the water before helping me step out. I watched him as he wrapped a towel around my cold frame before placing one around his waist.

"I'll go get you some clothes from your room. Stay here," he said. I nodded and followed him with my eyes as he walked out of the bathroom and shut the door behind him.

When he came back, he dressed me before dressing himself. He then carried me to our bed, where he laid me down right beside him with my eyes looking up to the ceiling while he was lying on his stomach with his arm around me.

"What's your mother's name?" I asked randomly. He looked over at me with curiosity very obvious on his features.

"Agnella," he answered.

"Agnella, Roberto, Alexandria, and our baby—four people who will always hold a special place in my heart and yours. I'm glad they're at peace and no longer in pain. Four names that I will never forget," I stated. Valentino was staring at me, still confused by what I was doing. "We deserve to be at peace too. There's a reason why we're still here. I'm done with crying my life away and calling things unfair because I'm doing nothing but wasting the life they never got to have. Let's not waste it anymore."

He leaned up to peer into my eyes before nodding his head. "I've been waiting for you to realize your worth to the world for as long as I've known you. I'm proud of you, Anastasia."

"I love you," I whispered.

"I love you most."

ANASTASIA

Seven months later

"$\mathcal{I}$ am really going to miss you guys," I told Orabella and her big baby bump.

She was going to name her baby boy Andrea, and I wished I could witness it all. That day after she was shot, she learned she was pregnant. It hurt to think about how we could've experienced everything at the same time, but Valentino helped me let that hurt go.

Her recovery was very fast. She was able to walk again in less than a month, seeing as the bullet didn't hit anything too major. Orabella was quick to forgive Valentino, and the same for Vincenzo.

Orabella placed one last small bag into the trunk of the car. It was the last day I would be seeing her. She didn't want to stay in the lifestyle Valentino and Vincenzo were born in, which I understood. I only wished I didn't have to miss so much with her gone.

"We will make sure to visit at every possible chance."

Orabella smiled. My shoulders fell as I looked at her. It was really going to be lonely without her there.

"You ready?" Vincenzo asked her, coming up and wrapping his arm around her.

"Yes," she gushed as he pressed his lips against her cheek.

I looked over at Valentino, who was watching them from a distance. I wondered if he was wishing the same thing I had been wishing, that it were us.

"See you soon," I told them before taking a few steps back.

Orabella waved happily before getting into the car with Vincenzo following behind her. With a frown, I watched as the car started up and they drove off down the road.

I watched them until the car disappeared from my sight. My shoulders fell before I turned on my heel and headed over to Valentino. He opened his arms out for me, leaving me to smile as I walked into them.

"Are you going to miss them?" I murmured against his chest.

"Of course I will, but I am glad you are still here with me," he answered. I pulled away from the hug to place a small peck on his lips.

"I'm ready to try for another baby," I said.

He furrowed his brows in confusion before grabbing my hand and placing a kiss on the backside of it.

"Are you sure?" he asked.

Nodding my head, I gave him a small smile. It was time for our happiness. I've wanted a baby since I lost ours, but I knew I wasn't ready. It had been months since the whole thing occurred, and now I knew I was finally ready.

"Well, let's not waste any more time," he said suggestively.

He led me into the house, where he opened the door to one of the guest bedrooms and pushed me in. A smirk quickly appeared on my face as I jumped into his arms with my legs wrapped around his waist. His lips were quick to meet mine and we battled for dominance. He won and slammed me against the wall rather harshly as his hand climbed up to my neck.

His hand began pinching my left nipple through my shirt while his other hand was inside my skirt and grabbing at my ass. The hand inside my skirt took hold of the waistband of my thong and began to pull it down. He always knew exactly what to do, which is why sex with him was always a bliss.

I slipped off my top and dropped it on the floor. Then, I took his hand and put it back on my breast. I heard him let out a small groan when he discovered I had no bra. I smiled at his reaction as his hands continued to push down my thong until it was completely off.

Next to come off was my miniskirt that he threw somewhere in the room. His left hand was now alternately mashing my breasts and pinching and pulling my nipples. Meanwhile, his other hand had pushed inside of me as he began to drive in and out. My body was on fire while one finger entered me and the others just massaged my clit. I reached down and found his crotch, where I felt his bulge straining against his pants. I held it as best as I could and rubbed it, feeling it getting bigger.

"Baby," he groaned.

I got down on my knees and quickly undid his slacks and pushed them down. His erection was long and thick, just perfectly in front of me underneath his boxers. He grabbed my hair and kept my face level with his cock. I pushed down his boxers and bit my lip at the sight of him.

I began to stroke it once it was free. I braced myself with my hand on his hip and gripped his shaft with my other hand. I began to jerk him off, slowly at first. When he pulled my hair back, I took that as my cue to stroke him faster and grip his cock tighter.

Soon, I started to blow him in earnest. My tongue swirled

around his shaft as I brought it into my mouth. Bringing his cock deep into my throat to the point I was at his base before I pulled back while running my tongue along the underside of it. Suddenly, I was bobbing my head faster and faster before I looked up at him. He let out a groan while tossing his head back and shutting his eyes. I sucked him gently, which resulted in me taking his whole shaft into my mouth once again. It went on like that for a few moments before he pulled me back up against the wall.

His hands went down to my pussy to test the waters, only to find out I was soaked. Giving him head always managed to leave me gasping for more. It turned me on to pleasure him, and he knew it.

Lining his erection up with my opening, he eased his cock inside me. My head rolled back when he pulled out slightly and thrust into me a little more. Once he was in, he grabbed my hands and pinned them to the wall.

"Go faster," I moaned.

He placed his lips against my skin, but instead of speeding up, he slowed down.

"Please," I begged, needing something more. He started to go faster and faster. My body was feeling intense as his cock began pummeling in and out of me at such a fast pace. My eyes were rolling in the back of my head while he managed to fuck me against the wall. I could even feel my toes curling while he pushed in and out of me, massaging my vaginal walls and coaxing me into an orgasm.

After a while, he let go of my hands and then lifted up one of my legs, followed by the other. He put them around his waist. He kept fucking me all the while. I tried to hold onto the wall but found there was nothing to grip, so I held onto his neck. His thrusts got deeper, faster, and harder. I began to shudder and squeeze around him. Suddenly, a loud moan ripped out of me as I came down onto his cock.

He chuckled against my skin before walking me over to the bed and throwing me down on top of it. He flipped my body over so that I was on my hands and knees. He didn't even give me a chance to think before he was inside of me again. My back arched instinctively while he thrust inside of me even faster.

My body was rocking against his, leaving the headboard to beat against the wall. After a while, I came again, while he came at the same time inside of me. He pulled out of me slowly before lying down right beside me.

After about two seconds he was kissing my neck once more.

"You aren't going to stop until I'm pregnant now, right?" I asked. He ignored my words completely and just used his hands to drag me on top of him.

"You got that right, Bambolina." He smiled.

Kissing his lips, I couldn't help the smile on my face.

"I never realized how much you've changed me in a positive way until now. Without you, I probably would've ended up just like my mum," I told him, thinking about my reaction in the club right after Alex died.

"You've changed me too," he said. I pecked his lips once more.

"Enough talking, Mr. Romano, let's get to fucking! *Woo*!" I exclaimed. He pulled away with a cringe on his face before shaking his head.

"Don't do that," he whispered. I narrowed my eyes at him before lightly slapping his chest. Loud laughter erupted from me at his words.

As soon as it died down, I stared up into his beautiful eyes, loving every bit of them.

"I love you, Anastasia." He smiled before bringing me back in to continue our kissing. "Now, let's get you pregnant," Valentino whispered.

"*Woo!*" I exclaimed.

THE END

EPILOGUE

ANASTASIA

*I*t was definitely not a *'woo'* experience. Being dressed in an all-white dress that looked so beautiful and elegant should've made me feel like a queen. I didn't feel like a queen at all. My belly was swollen with a baby girl and I couldn't help feeling nervous.

As I stared at myself in the full-length mirror, my hand rubbed my giant baby bump. There was a frown on my face as I looked at myself. I was marrying the man I loved with all of my heart, I was going to have a baby, and I should feel like the happiest person in the world—why was I so scared?

"Are you okay?" Orabella asked, coming into the room with Sarah.

"Yeah, I just…"

Suddenly, I began to cry. I tried my best to not mess up my makeup, but it was already too late. Everything was going to change after this, and I knew it.

"Sarah, can you go get her mom?" Orabella asked before walking over to me and bringing me into her embrace.

She held me tightly as she rubbed my back up and down.

"Don't cry. If you want, I'll go steal Vincenzo's keys and we can make a run for it," she said, her eyes widening.

I chuckled slightly before shaking my head and grabbing her arm.

"I want to marry him. I really, really do. I am so scared, but I don't even know why!" I sobbed.

Orabella burst out laughing while I cried into her shoulder. I was being so serious, but she must've thought I was joking.

"Orabella, I'm being serious!" I cried harder.

"It's just your pregnancy hormones. Don't worry, I've had them." She chuckled. I pushed her slightly, leaving her to laugh harder.

When the door opened, my mother and Orabella's baby boy, Andrea, walked into the room. He looked so handsome in his little suit that it brought a smile onto my face. My mother came up to me and gave me a huge hug before kissing my cheek.

"Look at me, I know you're nervous. I promise that when you walk down that aisle and you see Valentino standing there, everything will gracefully fall into the place. All of your worries will disappear. You're my strong little baby, I know you can do this," my mum said. I smiled at her before nodding my head and wrapping my arms around her once more.

Andrea began playing with my dress, leaving me to look down to see his arms stretched out wide for me. I pulled away from my mother before bending down to pick him up. I pecked his cheek, leaving a bit of lipstick on him. He giggled before wrapping his small arms around my neck.

"He likes you." Orabella laughed.

I sat him down on the floor, leaving him to run off toward his mother. A smile made its way onto my face as I turned to look back at my own mum.

"Can you help me fix my makeup?" I laughed. She smiled at me before sitting me down on the chair directly in front of a mirror.

"I'll go make sure everything is ready for you to come out. By the way, you look very beautiful," Orabella stated before walking over to me and smiling at me through the mirror. I returned her smile and then watched as she left with Andrea chasing after her.

"I've only been married once and that was to Alexandria's father." She smiled at the memory before wiping away the mess of makeup underneath my eyes thanks to my crying. I didn't say anything and just allowed her to continue talking. "I was crying too. Truthfully, you're lucky. You have a very handsome man who really loves you, and he would do anything to keep you happy. I couldn't say the same for the man I married. I should've realized he wasn't for me when I walked down the aisle to see he was high as a kite. Then, he introduced me to drugs, and I found them to be the love of my life."

I looked into her eyes and could see the heartbreak in them. My mother had a very hard life, and I was happy Alex made me promise to help her get to where she is now.

"I'm so proud of you, Mom," I told her as she reapplied my mascara.

She choked back a sob, leaving me to open my eyes.

"No, honey, I'm so proud of you," she said.

Standing up from the chair, I embraced her in a hug once more. All of our emotions escaped into the small embrace that sealed our mother-daughter bond. I loved her and she loved me. Now, there were no factors getting in the way.

After she finished my makeup, I stood in front of the full-length mirror to gawk at myself once more. I did look really pretty as a smile made its way onto my face.

"You look stunning." My mother smiled behind her tears.

I smiled brightly at her. Thankfully, since I was pregnant, I got to walk down the aisle barefoot. The gown was long enough to do so seeing as no one could see my feet. It was a tight white dress that left a long trail of white silk cloth behind me. It was beautifully elegant.

"Hey, it's time." Orabella smiled.

I let out a long exhale before following her out the door. There was loud chatter happening on the other side of the huge double doors before the bridal music began to play. I couldn't stop the nervous smile on my face as I turned to look at Orabella.

Then, Valerio walked up to me with his elbow ready for me to take.

"You're walking me down the aisle?" I asked, the urge to cry was quick to take over my emotions once more. I'd always wondered who would walk me due to the absence of my father.

"Of course, I wouldn't let my Barbie go all on her own." He smiled. The flower girl stepped slowly down the aisle, followed by all of the groomsmen, who were paired with Orabella, along with Liliana and Janice. My bridesmaids smiled at me as they began to walk down the aisle. After just a few seconds, I knew it was going to be my turn.

"I'm happy for you, my little block of cheese," Alex said like she was suddenly standing right beside me. "You look beautiful, you're going to have a baby, and most of all, you're marrying a man who loves you. You never needed me, you only needed to believe in yourself."

I could feel my eyes blurring as I looked at my imaginative Alex. "You need to let me go. I have always loved you, my banana, but now you love yourself enough for the both of us."

"Goodbye, Alex. I love you," I whispered softly.

Valerio looked at me with a small smile just as the doors opened. My eyes were quick to look at Valentino, who seemed just as nervous as me. Valerio and I walked in slow strides toward the altar with my smile never leaving my face. As we were walking, my eyes were brimming with tears of joy.

We continued down the aisle until we finally made it to the altar, where Valerio kissed my cheek.

"Who gives this woman to this man in marriage?" the priest asked.

Valerio glanced at me before taking my right hand and placing it into Valentino's.

"I do," he answered.

I smiled at him once more, feeling so thankful to have met him. He then took my left hand and placed it in Valentino's as well after I had passed my bouquet to my maid of honor—Orabella.

Valerio then turned and walked over to sit at the front, leaving me to gaze into the beautiful eyes of Valentino. He smiled at me and I happily returned it.

"You are so damn gorgeous," he mouthed.

"Welcome, everyone. Valentino Romano and Anastasia Smith have chosen you, those special and important to them, to witness and celebrate the beginning of their life together. Today, as they join in marriage, they also create a new bond and new sense of family—one that will undoubtedly include all who are present here today," the priest began.

My heart was thumping wildly in my chest and all I could think about was how badly I wanted to have sex with Valentino at that moment. *Bloody pregnancy hormones.*

"May you always need one another; not to fill an emptiness, but to help each other know your fullness. May you want one another; not out of lack, but to feel the warmth of their touch. May you embrace one another; not to encircle one another, but to give comfort. May you succeed in all important ways with each other, and not fail in the little graces. May you have happiness, and may you find it in making one another happy. May you have love, and always find love, in the pursuit of loving one another," the priest stated. His words meant a lot more to me than I thought they would, it described our entire journey.

"You may begin your vows," the priest told Valentino. He flashed his million-dollar smile before staring at me.

"I have never respected a woman as much as I have respected you. For a person who had to go through probably as many battles as I have, and still managed to become a woman our baby girl would admire, is hard to comprehend. I knew it from the day I saw you with that look in your eyes that said, *'I'm not working to feed me, I'm working to feed everyone.'* I didn't realize then that the woman I would quickly grow to love had to have that mentality of a warrior, who put others' needs before her own. Even as I look into your beautiful blue eyes now, I still see that innocence you never let the world ruin. I thank you for practically pinching me until I got down on my knee to ask you to marry me—" He was cut off by the laughter of our guests. My eyes were blurring in tears as I chuckled at his words. "It's exactly what I needed. I needed someone who would push me, and it was you. There is no other woman in the world that I could imagine spending the rest of my life with."

"Anastasia," the priest prompted.

I sniffled my tears before nodding my head.

"My life hasn't been easy, and you know that. What made me fall in love was the moment I got to see the real you and realize there was more to you than what you let on. No matter how many times I told myself to leave, or no matter how many times you pushed me away—I always made my way right back. It was meant to be us from the beginning, and even though I hate the events that led up to me meeting you, I'm glad it happened. My life is better with you in it. You are my outlet, and I am yours. I'm happy to push you to better yourself just like I'm happy that you're my guiding hand to lead me to greatness. The father of my child, the man of my heart—I love you. I love you so much, and that love will last forever."

"Aw!" everyone gushed.

My cheeks tinted a light pink color.

Then, little Andrea wobbled up to the altar with the ring. As he walked up to us, he touched my bottom, leaving everyone to start laughing once more.

Valentino narrowed his eyes at him before grabbing the ring from his baby hands. Andrea smiled innocently at him before running back down and into his mother's arms.

"I, Valentino, give you, Anastasia, this ring, as an eternal symbol of my love and commitment to you," he said before sliding the ring onto my finger. I smiled at it happily, seeing the beautiful diamond shine in the light.

Then, I grabbed his ring from Orabella before presenting it to him. "I, Anastasia, give you, Valentino, this ring, as an eternal symbol of my love and commitment to you."

"And now, by the power vested in me by the State of New York, I hereby pronounce you husband and wife. You may kiss your bride!"

Valentino hurriedly grabbed my ass and pulled me in for a kiss. Everyone quickly cheered as he kissed me harder. My hand wrapped around his neck, leaving him to deepen the kiss.

"Ladies and gentlemen, family and friends, I present to

you Mr. and Mrs. Anastasia and Valentino Romano!" he exclaimed.

* * *

I CHANGED from my wedding dress into a smaller gown. It was still tight, but it was less itchy than the wedding dress. My eyes traveled around to see everyone dancing and having the times of their lives. It was such a great sight to even see my mother, who was laughing and looking the happiest I had seen her in a long time.

Valentino walked up to me and wrapped his arm around my waist. "Come on, Mrs. Romano, I believe you owe me a dance."

He turned me around, so my back faced him and rubbed my belly. I smiled and nodded my head before taking his hand.

"A private dance, Mr. Romano?" I asked, thinking about the time we first met. "I believe it's going to cost you ten grand."

"As long as you open your legs," he whispered. Laughing, I grabbed his hand and dragged him over to the dance floor.

Happy. I was happy.

ABOUT THE AUTHOR

A. Marie is known for her mafia romance. Born and raised in Texas, she has a deep love for southern food and burgers. She always has her head buried in a book. Her favorite genres to read are dark romance, thrillers, mystery, and young adult fiction books. Her all-time favorite hobbies besides reading, is working out and writing.

A. Marie began writing at a very young age, and she has only grown to develop a deeper passion for it. She began writing on a platform called Wattpad, where she got to know so many amazing readers. Many of them still follow her journey today, and she couldn't be more appreciative for every single person.

Website:
Home | A. Marie (amarieauthor.org)

Facebook group:
http://www.facebook.com/groups/833653390722187/

BEFORE YOU GO...

Would you like to be a part of our *FREEBIE FRIDAY LIST* and get **6 FREE eBooks** and other *exclusive* sales sent to your inbox every Friday?

One email every week packed with bookish goodies!

We send out different genres such as Romance, Suspense, Thriller, Westerns, Paranormal, New Adult, and much more! If you'd like to join over 53,000+ subscribers, click below to be a part of FREEBIE FRIDAY...

Join FREEBIE FRIDAY!

https://limitlesspublishing.leadpages.co/freebiefriday/

Printed in Great Britain
by Amazon